Two Hearts Torn...

Danita Turner-Williams

La Faveur de Dieu
Petersburg, VA

La Faveur de Dieu Publishing
"God's favor"
Petersburg, VA 23804

ISBN: 978-0-9972800-6-7

Email Author at: danita.turner72@gmail.com

Visit our website: www.danitaturnerwilliams.com

Cover design courtesy of: Turner Concepts

Acknowledgements

First and foremost, I would like to thank God for entrusting me with the gift of writing. I praise you for you are the breath of life I breathe! I never imagined I would be an author until I received the yearning to begin writing and here is the finished product! I would like to thank my parents Edward and Yvonne Turner. I love you and you gave me the perfect gift of life. It is because of you I am the person that I am today. Mom, thank you for being my cheerleader and sharing the importance of birthing my gift to the world. To my siblings Karlos, Eddie, and Luke Turner, thanks for being there as I shared parts of this journey with you. Thank you for your feedback and your encouragement. To my husband Charlie Williams, III, thank you for the countless hours of support you yielded to me and for being such an intricate part of my journey. To my dear friends Linda Jefferson, Pearl Pulley, and David Moore, thank you for the countless times you sat and listened to the story unfolding, holding on to every word and asking questions regarding the fate of the characters. I appreciate the words you spoke into my life and spirit. To my editor Karen Rodgers, thank you for the countless hours you put into making sure that my baby had all of the nourishment needed to sustain life!

Chapter 1

"Hey baby, how are you?"

"Missing you! How are you?"

"Feeling the same."

Fernando had to talk softly as his wife lay beside him. He was so used to her lying there, being ignorant of how to fulfill his needs. Oh, how he longed for the day he would hold Sugar in his arms again.

"Are you there?" Sugar asked.

"Yeah, I'm just thinking about you, baby, and how I long for your touch."

Sugar was married to the pastor of their church, Alpha and Omega Community Church and she lived with her husband and two children, Akeem and Jessica. *It's really difficult living in a loveless marriage, and more of a strain having the position as first lady of a church.* Sugar knew that things were moving downhill when she discovered that she no longer desired her husband. A husband should be more than the warmth of a body lying beside you. Being married and still having feelings of loneliness and emptiness was far from the life of matrimony she'd anticipated. So many nights she had to bring herself to ecstacy; longing for the touch of another but to no avail...

Remembering Fernando... "So when are we going to see each other again?" Sugar asked.

"As soon as I can get away," Fernando stated softly. He moved from under the covers and quickly moved them back before the fresh, cool breeze of the night air disturbed the sleep of his wife Brenda. She looked so peaceful lying there, which was so far from the person she had become. Brenda had a very cold character; it appeared like she didn't care for the well-being of anyone other than herself. Fernando remembered when he first met Brenda approximately fifteen years ago and how it seemed she was the answer to his prayers. They married about 18 months after their initial meeting. Fernando envisioned Brenda being beautiful and attentive to all of his needs. They would laugh and it seemed that they could talk for hours. The two of them possessed the unique ability to complete each other's sentences. It seemed that they were so in tune to each other. Nowadays it seemed as though they couldn't be in each other's presence for thirty minutes without having a disagreement, or more of a verbal altercation. *What has happened to us?*

"Fernando," called Sugar.

As he answered, "Yes," he reflected that his name sounded so sweet as it left Sugar's soft lips.

"I really need to see you, I miss your touch and more importantly, there are many things that I need to share with you," Sugar stated.

"Baby, are you okay? Do you need to talk to me now?" Fernando questioned.

"No, there's not enough time now, but I will be in touch very soon. Have a good night's sleep and we will meet up very soon," Sugar said.

"So before we end the call I have been meaning to tell you how much I feel your childhood name Sugar is so befitting of your character. That is why it is important that we take into consideration how our names actually brand us as individuals."

"Aww, sweetie, thanks. I appreciate your kind words and yes, we definitely live up to our names."

"Alright, I will be waiting for your call. Bye for now," Fernando stated softly as he was wondering what she needed to discuss with him face to face. Sugar broke through the silence, "Bye."

Fernando walked around the room for a few minutes in silence, still wondering... *It must be unfavorable news that my dear Sugar has to relay.* He reflected on the time when he was fifteen years old and his parents wanted to talk with him face-to-face, only to inform him that they were getting a divorce. That news seemed to shatter his life and was very difficult for him to digest at the time. He remembered questioning them, "What did I do to cause you to make this drastic decision? I make good grades, I am athletic and I try to make y'all proud of me." His mom stated, "Son, you had nothing to do with our decision; it's best for us that we separate, but this doesn't change the love that we have for you, son."

"Fernando," a distant voice called. It was Brenda, and she could call out with the most cold tone, which irritated Fernando to no end.

"Yes," answered Fernando.

"What are you doing and why are you not in bed?" questioned Brenda.

"Just thinking. I'm about to come now," Fernando responded.

Brenda stormed into *Beautiful Diva's*—her place of business, her baby, her world—slamming the door behind her. Brenda always seemed to make her presence known everywhere she went and she had an air that she should be catered to.

"Sally, hun, would you fetch me a towel out of the utility area and tell my 1:00 that I'm ready for her?" She snarled at the shampoo girl in her normal demeaning way.

Sally humbly walked to the adjoining room to let Ms. Nelly know that she was expected by her highness. Sally wondered how long she would have to suffer working for such an ungrateful, rude, person. She thought Brenda looked right through her, as if she was no one, or someone who was beneath Brenda. God said when he created us we were made in the likeness of Him and... 'It was good.'

Ms. Nelly approached Brenda's chair. "How are you doing, Brenda?"

"I'm doing ok, just a little rushed," she stated with much agitation. "I'll be glad when I don't have to perform such manual labor; it's so beneath me!"

stated Brenda. "A woman of my stature should not have to perform such tasks," she continued.

Ms. Nelly responded, "The Lord will provide, he always makes a way."

Brenda rolled her eyes and her anger intensified as Ms. Nelly mentioned God. "Where was God when I needed Him, while my mother was lying on her sick bed, dying from cancer?" she raised her tone of voice. "My mother put all her trust and confidence in a God that didn't deliver. She prayed and she told me that God would deliver her. I even prayed and God didn't answer my prayers, so why would I trust Him to make a way?"

Ms. Nelly was a Licensed Clinical Social Worker and a Crisis Minister at her church, so she was deeply touched by the pain she heard in Brenda's voice.

"Wow," stated Ms. Nelly, "that must have been a great deal of pain that you went through with your mother. Do you want to talk about it further?"

"No, I don't want to talk about it anymore," she snapped.

Ms. Nelly stated, "Just know that I am here if you need me."

"Alright, but for now, let's concentrate on how you want your hair styled."

Chapter 2

"Let the church say Amen," shouted Pastor Spickley from the pulpit.

As he stood facing the congregation, Sugar braced herself for what he would say next. She reflected back on his sermon about a year ago when he stood and announced to the congregation, "My wife isn't fulfilling her wifely duties, and it has been a year since I have had home cooking." She'd pondered why her husband would be so inconsiderate of her needs and what she required as a woman and wife. She remembered how some of the sisters of the congregation came to her after church and scolded her for not cooking for her husband. "Don't you know that you are supposed to cook for him and be submissive to him?" Mother Clary told her with conviction. The older mothers of the church always had a way of shifting their weight! Out of respect for Mother Clary's age, Sugar had made no comments back to her.

Sometimes it really disgusts me how a woman can be so insensitive to another woman when she is down and out, Sugar mused. *Yes, it was at that time that things began to shift in the Spickley home. After that announcement every Sunday the sisters would take turns coming over to prepare a meal for my husband. As they entered the house they would say that they wanted to make sure the "pastor is taken care of." I wonder which sister will be coming today after church. I certainly hope that it's not Sister Candy as she always adds a little sugar to the meal. Candy makes sure that her dress is a bit short just over her knees and she always seems to be a bit clumsy as she drops a spoon or fork which causes her to bend over so gingerly to pick it up.*

Sugar's attention returned to the sermon as Pastor Spickley was tapping the microphone, "Are we all here?" he stated with agitation... looking directly at Sugar. *He has a condescending way of looking at me... better yet, through me.*

"Today's message comes from the book of Genesis. Yes, today we are going to have a word from the beginning. From the beginning of creation, God has loved man and wanted the best for man, he even created woman for him. Everything was peaceful as they were running around naked in the garden. Then the woman ate of the fruit that God instructed her not to eat and she gave it to the man and this began the fall of man. Now, church I wonder what would have happened had the serpent presented the fruit to the virile man? Would it have been accepted or rejected?

I feel within my heart of hearts it would have been rejected. The Bible says, the woman is the weaker vessel, so that's why the serpent tempted her."

For the next hour Sugar watched as Pastor Spickley ranted and raved walking across the pulpit and across the altar, and then down the aisle preaching. She began to turn a deaf ear to this sermon also. *It seems that there is no variety in his style of preaching.* She reflected on a conversation held with her husband. "*Honey, don't you think that your sermons are demeaning to women?*" He looked *at me with such disgust and stated, "So, now you are higher than God? I'm supposed to listen to you, instead of the voice of the Lord?*"

"*Well,*" I continued, "*from my Bible reading God doesn't always scold the people, he has compassion as well.*"

"Well Sugar, that's your interpretation and I have mine, and that will be the final word of this conversation," he'd scolded.

The phone rang and it seemed that it was a million miles away, Sugar thought she was dreaming as it began ringing louder and louder. Sugar answered in a muffled voice, sounding as if a frog was croaking, "Hello."

"Yes, hello, this is Nurse Kelly calling from Dr. Peters' office. May I speak with your mother, Akeem?"

"Kelly, this is Sugar."

"Oh, I'm sorry girl, I must have woke you. Sugar, I wanted to call you to be the first to congratulate you."

"Congratulate me?" Sugar paused. "Why are you congratulating me?"

"Well, Sugar when you were seen last week and we ran the blood work for your physical... well, it shows in the report that you are pregnant," Kelly shouted with excitement.

"What? Pregnant? there must be some mistake!" screamed Sugar.

Kelly was apologetic, "I thought you would be happy about this news. I know that you have two children already, but God has smiled on you once again."

Sugar tried to contain herself as she ended the conversation... "Thanks for calling with this news; I'll talk to you later."

"Sugar, before you hang up, don't forget to schedule your prenatal care."

"Ok, I… uh will, bye," Sugar responded.

Sugar was distraught, almost dispondent. *What am I going to do? Pregnant now, with another child? I wonder how far into the pregnancy I am.* Thoughts continued to swarm around in her head as Stanley Spickley entered the room from the bathroom. "Who was that on the phone?" he questioned.

"It was Dr. Peters' office calling concerning my test results."

"And…?" He motioned for more.

"And they said that all of the results were within normal limits."

"Why did it seem that you were excited as if it wasn't favorable news?" he demanded.

"Well, I was excited that all is well, and that God continues showering blessings on the Spickley family," Sugar stated sarcastically.

"Alright," Stanley snapped, "well I'm going out."

Sugar's mind began to spin around a million miles per hour. This was the way that Stanley always exited the home, stating he was going out, never explaining where he was heading. Sugar didn't acknowledge it this time, she was preoccupied with her new found information.

Sugar felt the need to talk; there were so many things that were going on and she really needed to gather her thoughts. She could always depend on her sister, Gloria, to assist her in ironing out issues. *I sure hope that she is home...*

"Hello, Gloria?"

"Hey Sugar, how is my favorite sister doing?"

"Not too well, sis," Sugar stated.

"What did Stanley do now; do I need to come over and set things in order?" Gloria questioned.

"Sis, I'm not in the position to discuss this over the phone; can you meet me at our favorite café for coffee?"

"Sure," Gloria stated, "I can be there in five."

"Great, see you then."

Sugar grabbed her coat and proceeded out the door only to see Akeem on the doorstep. "Akeem, what's going on, honey? Why are you sitting on the doorstep?"

"I missed the bus and I didn't know how to tell you."

"Ah, Akeem, I am rushing and need to meet your Aunt Gloria now," Sugar replied sharply. "Alright, I have no choice but to drop you off at school on my way. Did you finish your science project?" Sugar investigated with much concern.

"Yes, ma'am, I was up until 12:00 a.m. putting the finishing touches on it, I sure hope that I get a good grade, because I really put a lot of time, energy and effort into it," Akeem responded.

Sugar smiled as she looked over at Akeem... *My baby has grown up right before my eyes.* She reflected back to the day that she was due to deliver Akeem, and as she lay waiting for his arrival, time passed by so quickly. She was told by the medical staff that her labor was over 18 hours, which made him a high risk delivery, and he had to be delivered by caesarean section. *Wow, that was seventeen years ago, he is almost a grown man, and will be heading off to college next year. Almost at the close of adolescence and soon will be transitioning into adulthood, and now… I'm pregnant.* The thoughts seemed to continue flowing in like a rushing wind during a windy winter day. Before she knew it tears were streaming down her face. She quickly swiped at them, hoping Akeem wouldn't notice.

As Sugar pulled into the driveway in front of the school, Akeem asked, interrupting her thoughts, "Mom, are you okay?"

"Yes, Akeem, I'm okay."

"It just seems like you have a lot on your mind, and I know that I don't tell you all the time, but I love you and you mean so much to me. I appreciate all that you and Dad have done to make provisions for me and Jessica."

"Akeem, I love and appreciate you too, and you have enriched my life more than you know. Right now, Mom is just passing through a tough time, but everything will be alright. Thank you for being concerned." As they embraced, Sugar said, "You better get to class, young man."

"Ok, Mom, I will see you this evening."

Sugar could hardly concentrate as she dialed Gloria's number as she headed to the café.

"Hey sis," Gloria answered in a worried tone, "where are you?"

"I'm sorry, Gloria, I ended up having to drive Akeem to school. He was sitting on the front stoop as I was leaving the house to meet you."

"Alright, I have secured us a nice, cozy, private spot in the back so that we can discuss this matter privately."

"I can always count on you, sis. I love you so much. I tell you, when I think of some of our crazy family members I sure am glad that God blessed me with such a dynamic sister."

"Why, sis, you are too kind." Gloria blushed.

Sugar arrived at the parking lot of the café, shaking as she gathered her keys, feeling overwhelmed, trying to hold it together without breaking down. It seemed as though so many emotions were racing at the same time, it was difficult for her to understand exactly what she was feeling: frustration, anger, sadness, bewilderment, just a collection of emotions that were all rushing through her mind at once.

"Hello, ma'am, how may I help you?" greeted the waitress at the café.

"Yes, I'm here meeting my—"

The waitress finished Sugar's sentence midstream. "Oh, I'll show you to your sister."

As I was approaching the table I realized I didn't know where to begin the conversation. What was happening to me? Why was it happening now? How did I get myself into this position? Am I being punished for having an extra-marital affair? All seemed like fair questions or thoughts swimming around in my head.

The waitress escorted Sugar to the back table in the corner where Gloria was nestled. Sugar recognized her from the beginning of the aisleway. *How could I miss her reddish orange ponytail? My sister is such a "queen." She always commands attention but not in arrogance. Almost regal. God has blessed me tremendously with a sister like her.*

As Sugar approached the table, Gloria stood up and came from around the table and greeted her as she always did. Gloria provided her sister with the warmest hug. She always did love on her big sister.

"Good morning, sis." Gloria smiled. *She has a smile that could light up the room. When I am in her presence I always feel a sense of ease, like nothing can touch me, so protected. Gloria always has my best interest at heart.*

"Good morning, sis," Sugar stated.

"Okay Sugar, I have taken the liberty of ordering you your favorite coffee, just the way you like it, with hazelnut creamer and eleven packs of sugar."

"Thanks, sis," Sugar said as she accepted the coffee. "So is this Cameroonian coffee, Costa Rican coffee, or another brand?" Sugar questioned while setting it on the table, removing her coat and taking her seat.

"Well, sis, you know they are a bit slow on making international coffees available, especially from the motherland. With that being said, I ordered you Costa Rican coffee," Gloria replied.

Sugar sipped her coffee slowly while taking in a deep breath as she collected her thoughts and brought Gloria up to speed. "Gloria, I received a very disturbing call this morning."

"What is it, sis?" Gloria paused, grabbing the edge of her seat as if she were in danger of falling off.

"I'm pregnant!"

"Oh no, sis, what happened? I thought you were on the pill and using protection."

"Yeah, I was, but don't you remember I had that upper respiratory infection about a month ago and received the antibiotics for it?"

"Yeah, and what does that have to do with anything?" Gloria interrupted.

"Well, it has everything to do with it as the antibiotics reduce the strength of the birth control pills."

"Oh no!" shouted Gloria, placing her hands over her mouth. "Was that during the time you were last with Fernando?"

"Yes, that's what's causing me to freak out. As you are aware, I cringe when Stanley touches me. It has been years since I've felt any connection with him, especially in the area of love. I don't understand how a man can seem to be so holy among his flock but have no love or benevolence to show his wife. I have been struggling in this loveless, unfulfilling marriage for far too long. When I hear his vehicle entering the driveway, Gloria, my spirits drop and I immediately feel depressed. I don't want to see him. I often wish that he wouldn't come home. I know that must sound awful to say about someone who you took vows with before a congregation of family, friends and before the Lord.

"When we married I thought that I would love Stanley forever. I felt that he completed me and would protect me… so I thought. Or maybe it was the fact that he said to me, 'Sugar, God told me you are my wife.' Well, I was thinking that I loved him and I saw no need to validate his remark, as God had spoken to him, and that was good enough for me. You know how we were raised in church and that we knew to wait for our husband to seek us out?"

"Yes," Gloria chimed in.

"I have been thinking that maybe I should have sought God for myself. Sis, I don't feel connected to Stanley at all. But with Fernando, I know that I am in love with him, I melt and all of my body feels alive the instant he touches me. With a stroke of his hand he seems to wash all my troubles away. His touch is so electric it travels from the top of my head throughout my body. It radiates in the pit of my stomach and the innermost part of my vaginal area... I have never felt like this before. He offers so much love and compassion, but it's not at all about the lovemaking alone. Although, I struggle with the fact that we are both married, and it's a sin for us to be together, I feel comfortable while I'm in his presence and while sharing intimacy. How can these feelings be wrong?

"I feel that Fernando truly completes me. Oh, sis, it seems that we connect on so many levels, mentally, physically, emotionally, spiritually, intellectually, financially, and sexually. These levels are important... Being reared under a spiritual leader we were taught not to 'be unequally yoked with unbelievers.' When dissecting this information, I realized just because Stanley is a believer doesn't mean he was supposed to be my husband. In marriage it should be a partnership and love alone isn't enough.

Gloria nodded vigorously.

"A couple with a connection on 7 levels: Spiritually, intellectually, emotionally, mentally, physically, financially, and sexually is practically unheard of. If a relationship is lacking on any of these levels, that lack can cause problems and leave room for an individual to be unfulfilled and unhappy. A couple should be two that move close to each other and continue to grow... If one grows and one stays stagnant, this causes issues that strain the relationship as well.

"With Stanley, I feel that we have grown stagnant in so many different areas, and as I look back, it began when he started making demeaning remarks about 17 years ago after the delivery of Akeem and I no longer had the Coke-bottle shape. He would call me a big elephant… 'Look at you, you look as though you swallowed a basketball with your stomach protruding out. Didn't you deliver the baby already?' He'd continue, 'I can't stand looking at you, you disgust me!' But sis, that's not the worst. The thing that cut me to the core, was the day he told me that he wanted me to keep my clothes on during our intimacy, because he could not stand to look at my flabby body! Did he even take into consideration what my body went through as I carried and delivered Akeem? Did he take into consideration how his remarks would make me feel? I could never say something so cruel to him; although, he doesn't look the same way that he did when we married 20 years ago I have never judged him."

"Whoa, sis, that is some really heavy stuff that you just shared," Gloria stated empathetically. "I knew that Stanley didn't treat you like the queen that you are; however, I didn't know that you were going through so much emotional and mental anguish. But, sis, God is still there, I know that He was the one that strengthened you to go through all of the heartache and pain that you have endured until this very moment. One thing for sure is that you must fulfill your destiny, your divine purpose that God has predestined. Although the road seems very bleak, I know that God will make it clearer for you as time goes on."

Gloria began to sing, "*By and by, when the morning comes.*"

Gloria had a song for everything, and every occasion. This song consoled Sugar's very spirit.

"Thanks, sis, I really needed that. I know that God has something greater for me; although, at this present time I really need Him to help me with this situation."

Chapter 3

"Hello, Fernando, how are you doing?"

"All is well with me, my love, how are things going for you?"

"Well," Sugar replied, then took a deep breath, "things are a bit overwhelming presently, and that's the nature of my call. I know a great deal of time has passed since we last spoke and I informed you that we needed to meet."

"Yes, Sugar, I recall that conversation and I have been anticipating our meeting," stated Fernando.

"When is it possible for us to meet?" Sugar asked.

"The ball is in your court as you have to make arrangements for your family; I don't have to cross as many hurdles as you do."

"Okay, that's true. What about next Wednesday, the 17th? We can meet in our usual place and I will arrange to spend the night."

"Okay, darling, that sounds really good. Sugar?"

"Yes, Fernando."

"How are things going for you?"

"Things are going okay, baby but there are some things that I have to share with you and I will feel better telling you these things face-to-face."

"Okay, understood. How are our children?"

"They are doing well, thanks for asking."

Sugar's heart usually filled and overflowed with joy when Fernando asked about her children, although they didn't belong to him. Fernando seemed to always appreciate her children and accept them as his, since they were a part of Sugar's DNA. *At this moment since I was feeling so overwhelmed, a sense of sadness entered my heart.*

"Well," Sugar stated, "I will see you on the 17th."

"Okay," Fernando stated, "the 17th it is; can't wait to see you, Charlotte."

"Fernando, why are you calling me by my government name?"

Fernando chuckled and hung up the phone.

Brenda called for Fernando as she entered the house. "Fernando, where are you? I have some packages that I need you to grab from the car."

Brenda wondered where he was. Brenda thought there were only a few things that Fernando was good for, and one of them was for him to be at her beck and call. She wondered why he always thought she wanted to talk to him. What would the conversation be? Brenda was only concerned about the hair salon that she was in the process of having renovated. She had it all planned out from the purchasing of booths, employing nail technicians, and massage beds for the spa. Things were beginning to unfold the way Brenda imagined, and she had worked so hard to get to this point.

Brenda celebrated being so close to reaching her successful end that she could smell it! She perceived what she had acquired was all due to the hard work, dedication and through the sweat of her brow! This was a wonderful feeling and sense of accomplishment for her. She reflected her mother would have been so proud of how things progressed. Brenda had anticipated seeing her standing in the entryway of the salon, smiling at her, telling her how proud she was of her. If only her mother could have seen the finished product.

Before Brenda realized it, tears were streaming down her face. Brenda was working for stability and having enough money for her later, greater years. "Fernando, are you here?" she hollered, traveling up the stairway leading to the bedroom. Fernando was lying on the bed fast asleep. "Fernando!" She yelled with such agitation.

"Huh, huh? Yeah, what's wrong?"

"I need you to get the packages out of the car for me!"

"What? You woke me up for that?"

"Yes, is there a problem?"

"Brenda, we have been over this so many times before, yet you continue being insensitive to my needs. I'm lying here sleeping and you have the audacity to wake me up to get some packages. If you think that I'm going to get out of this bed now as tired as I am, you are wrong!" Fernando was furious. "Now, if you don't mind, I am going back to sleep!" He turned over and was drifting off to sleep as he heard Brenda stomping out of the room, slamming the bedroom door, and stomping down the stairs. He was awakened. "What the hell are you good for?" yelled Brenda.

Fernando couldn't believe her; He was getting very tired of trying to be reasonable with Brenda when she continued being unsympathetic to his needs. He didn't understand how she could feel that it's okay to awaken him for something as trivial as that. Fernando wondered if this is all there was to being married. One thing that gave him consolation was the thought of wrapping Charlotte…his sweet, sexy Sugar in his arms and making sweet love to her. Somehow that seemed to provide Fernando with what he needed at that precise moment to move on.

Fernando reasoned within himself, how could he not love and appreciate someone that gave him so much love and compassion. Everyone desires to be shown that they are appreciated. It had been a long time since he felt love or appreciation from Brenda. He often wondered how things turned out so badly between him and Brenda. Things seemed to shift drastically in their marriage when Brenda's mother lost her battle with cancer six years ago. Brenda would often converse with Fernando and inform him of all the new treatments the doctors were proposing. Fernando remembered so clearly when Brenda came home one evening and she said she really needed to talk. Fernando fixed them both coffee as they cuddled on the couch.

Brenda stated to Fernando, "Babe, the doctors are at a standstill with my mother's treatment. They say that she has an infection in her blood and the cancer is spreading so rapidly that they are unable to treat the infection as quickly as it is reproducing." She continued, "The doctors are stating one option of combating the cancer is to have a bone marrow transplant. We all need to be tested and hopefully there will be a match."

"I know that God is able to work this situation out; the doctors have given their report, but we shall believe the report of the Lord," Fernando told her optimistically. They touched and agreed in prayer concerning the situation, leaving it in the hands of God. We then smiled knowing that God would work it out. It seemed that things were going well at that moment. After that night, approximately six months later, they were called in to the Intensive Care Unit and the doctors reported that Brenda's mom wouldn't make it through the night. *I remember it all so vividly, it seemed it was happening in slow motion.* Brenda questioned, "Why is this happening? I thought you assured me that God would deliver her!" Brenda yelled.

"Brenda, calm down, take some deep breaths, we have to continue to believe," Fernando tried to reassure her. *That night, I lost my mother-in-law and my wife.* Fernando believed it was as though Brenda blamed him for the death of her mother. Fernando was surprised when Brenda told him she thought he had power in his prayers, and that God would hear his prayers. Brenda let him know in no uncertain terms that she was mistaken about him.

"Well, you can have that God of yours, because he can't be so just since He allowed my mother to be taken away from me. My mother was the only one who truly loved and understood me." Then she burst into tears...

Fernando tried to console Brenda but it was as though she had a heart that was cold as ice. For some reason he wasn't able to penetrate her stony heart. According to the Word of God, our heart contains the "issues of life." All our thoughts, feelings and emotions are contained in our hearts, which control the way we act. When I think of how Brenda's heart moved from being loving and supportive to being controlling and lacking compassion, Fernando wondered what shifted in Brenda's heart? While thinking of the processes of Brenda's heart, a scripture came to his mind: "A good man, out of the good treasure of his heart brings forth that which is good, and an evil man out of the evil treasure of his heart brings forth that which is evil, for out of the abundance of the heart the mouth speaks" (Luke 6:45).

"Lord, God it's true that you know all the things that abide in my heart, the good, the bad, and the ugly; I am transparent in your sight. I ask that you lead me in the right direction concerning all aspects of my life. It appears that my life is in shambles but you are able to work within the shambles. I ask for forgiveness of my sins, and ask to be received into your fold. Amen," Fernando prayed earnestly. "I understand and am aware of some of the issues of my life, that I am married to Brenda, and that I am involved in an intimate relationship outside of my marriage." Looking up at the ceiling, toward the sky, he continued, "But God you know that I love Charlotte, and it's hard for me to walk away from her. God, you see what I am going through with Brenda and you also know that this has turned into a loveless marriage." Fernando looked forward to the 17th; he couldn't wait until he could lay his eyes on Charlotte and fully behold all of her beauty. To him her beauty was evident both inside and out. *What a wonder to behold!*

As Fernando's thought was completed, Brenda entered the room.

"Oh, so I see that sleeping beauty has awakened from his sleep," Brenda stated sarcastically.

Fernando didn't even give Brenda the pleasure of responding to her sly remark. "I was thinking that we need to seek counseling if we are interested in salvaging our marriage," Fernando stated emphatically.

"Well, why do you feel that we need to seek counseling? I know that I don't have a problem, perhaps you should get individual counseling," Brenda snapped.

"Okay Brenda, it appears I need to spell it out for you since you seem to be in denial that our relationship isn't in perfect standing. I suggest that you think about the importance of having a professional to intervene and offer us help," stated Fernando. "Brenda, it appears that you have changed so drastically over the last few years of our marriage! When was the last time that we sat down and had a conversation?" he questioned, yearning for her to realize that there was something going wrong in their marriage.

"Before we were married, Brenda, you pursued me and made me feel needed, not just wanted," stated Fernando. "Do you realize that every time I try to open up to you to address my needs, you constantly push me away?"

Brenda's anger intensified, "Blah, blah, blah, this is all I hear from you. Do you realize that I'm trying to build a business and at this point that is my only concern? Why are you being so emotional? I mean, really are you on the rag?" Brenda shouted.

"Brenda," Fernando called her name softly, "do you realize that God was the one that made it possible for your business to blossom?"

"Please, Fernando I don't have time for that religious stuff! Why is everyone throwing religion in my face? All of the business contracts and bank notes read BRENDA STORM!"

"That's another thing that has been ailing me, why didn't you accept my last name?"

"Really Fernando, why have you been pondering that? Why would I want to bear the name Sexton? Have you bumped your head? Storm has more meaning and more relevance to my personality. Now back to my prior statement: The reason is because all of my accomplishments have been made due to the sweat of *my* brow, *my* hard work! So please do me a favor and keep that God stuff to yourself!" Then she stormed off.

Chapter 4

Jessica entered the great room where Sugar rested on the couch reading the daily newspaper.

"Hey Mom, how are you?"

"I'm doing well, just reading this depressing news! Why are there so many negative things printed here? I often wonder why the reporters seem to only dwell on negative things to report? Is it that people have itching ears that desire negative reports over positive ones?" Sugar said, processing loudly.

"Mom, I have no idea," Jessica stated.

"That's alright, Princess, your mom was only venting. Nevertheless, how are you doing?"

"Mom, I'm doing great, but a little nervous, what should I expect at the prom? I still need to pick out my dress. Are we still going shopping this week; you know the prom is on Friday, the 12th?"

"Yes, Jessica, I'm aware as I agreed I will be taking you on Thursday to the boutique."

"Mom, is that going to give us enough time? I want to be sure that I have the cutest dress, along with the perfect accessories."

"Jessica we have enough time, don't worry! I know how particular you are and how worried you get."

"Mom, if I ask you something do you promise not to get angry?"

"Yes, Jessica you know that you can talk to me about whatever is on your mind."

"Well, Mom I was wondering what is going on with you and Dad? You don't seem as happy as you were before and I noticed that the past few nights you all have been sleeping apart. Mom, I also heard you crying in the bathroom this morning. Is everything okay?"

"Jessica, there is nothing that you need to worry about. Your father and I are just going over a small hurdle and need some time apart. Don't you worry about it, let's prepare for Thursday evening when we have our ladies' day outing in preparation for the prom."

"Ok." Jessica smiled.

Wow, Sugar thought, *my little girl is growing up right before my eyes.* That brought a smile to Sugar's face.

"Mom, why are you smiling?"

"Well, princess, you always have a way of brightening up my day."

"Mom, are Aunt Gloria and my cousin Jael still joining us for our ladies' day outing on Thursday?"

"Of course!" Sugar stated excitedly.

"Good," stated Jessica. "I always enjoy spending time with my auntie and cousin."

"So do I. Have you already set the table?"

"Yes, Mom that's the other reason I came in here, to let you know everything is set."

"Ok, great. Let Akeem and your dad know that dinner is ready."

"Ok, Mom I'm about to do it now."

As Sugar entered the kitchen to gather the food that she prepared for dinner tonight, she noticed

Stanley standing at the head of the table. This was so like him feeling that he deserved such special attention.

"How are you doing, Sugar? I called you earlier today and you didn't answer the phone." he stated, agitated.

Sugar took in a very deep breath. *Here we go again. Can't he leave well enough alone? Does he even know how much it has taken out of me to prepare dinner tonight, and still include him after what happened last night? He just doesn't seem to have a clue. Did he really think that I was going to let him into my bed when he had the nerve to come in after 2:00 a.m. this morning? Who does he think he's fooling? He came into the bedroom with an excuse that the church meeting extended until about 10:00 p.m. after which all the board members decided to go out for dinner. Who is serving dinner until 2:00 a.m.? He told me that they were at the restaurant until*

12:00 a.m. and then there was a member that was having many personal issues that needed counseling which couldn't wait until the morning. I questioned him early this morning: Was your phone not working? Why didn't you call and alert me to the issues of your evening? So many emotions were flowing through Sugar's head. *Why do I continue with this marriage? Is it worth salvaging?*

"Charlotte," Stanley called, "what's wrong? Are you still angry?" he questioned.

"Stanley,what do you think? I am still trying to process what happened. Let me have my space!" Sugar yelled. Her anger intensified to the point that her legs and hands were shaking, making it known how she hated that feeling of discord and distance. Sugar lived for tranquility and calmness, she didn't like when there were unresolved issues. She rushed out of the kitchen into the adjoining bedroom and tried to calm down. As she went into the bedroom and turned to close the door, there was Stanley standing in the doorway.

"Sugar, please, let's talk."

"Stanley, I don't have the strength to talk, leave me alone!" she screamed.

Stanley left the room. Sugar's anger intensified and she was crying now because she was furious. Sugar called her sister, Gloria.

"Hey sis," answered Gloria. "Sis... sis?" She wasn't hearing anything. "Are you there, Charlotte? Charlotte," Gloria called.

"Yes, I'm here."

"What's bothering you?"

"Sis, please come and pick me up," she was able to utter in between the tears. Gloria could feel the pain through the phone. She hated with a passion when her sister reached this point.

"I'll be there in five!"

"I'll be waiting on the veranda for you."

"Ok, see you soon," stated Gloria.

Sugar headed out of the bedroom; she took her coat from the closet and headed out the door. As she was about to open the door, Stanley was standing beside her. Sugar didn't understand why Stanley was standing there once again intruding into her personal space.

"Charlotte, where do you think you're going?" questioned Stanley. "We haven't finished our discussion! We need to talk this out," he insisted.

"Stanley," she stated in a calm voice, almost a whisper, "I have done all the talking with you I plan to for the evening and I suggest that you not wait up for me."

From where Sugar stood she could see the headlights of Gloria's car entering the driveway.

Sugar ran out into the driveway as she saw Gloria's car. Sugar entered Gloria's car bursting into tears.

Gloria could hardly contain herself, "Sis, what did that donkey do this time?"

Sugar gasped in between the tears and stated, "It's a combination of things that he continues doing. My heart is hurting, I feel like he is literally cutting my heart to shreds!" she managed to get out. "Sis, I was so angry tonight that I had to contain myself. I felt like punching him right in his face, right between his eyes!"

"Sugar, this is so unlike you; I know that you like things to be calm and mellow, this is definitely out of character for you. What brought you to this point?" Gloria responded anxiously.

"Well, sis, he decided to stay out until 2:00 this morning and didn't have the courtesy to call and inform me of his whereabouts. Problems have just been building and building. It's just like that balloon that you continue to blow air in or the Pepsi Cola that you shake up and then pop the top. What happens in both instances? It explodes! That's what has happened to us; it all began when he announced to the congregation that I wasn't performing my wifely duties."

"What? You can't be serious! I know that was painful."

"Yes, sis, but that's not the half of it. Each Sunday one of the sisters comes over to the house to prepare a meal for my husband. How do you think that makes me feel? It makes me feel incomplete, like I don't have all of the ingredients to meet his taste in food preparation. When the sisters serve him his food, they set his place and treat him like a King. Sister Candy had the audacity to spoon feed him right in front of me. There is absolutely *no respect*!

"Furthermore, he has been changing the amount of money that he has deposited into our joint checking account. It appears he is putting away about $1,000 a month that he doesn't account for. Where is he putting this money, taking it from our house and children? Gloria, you know that I don't wish any ill will to my husband. All of my money, except a small amount, goes into paying the bills and when there isn't enough, then I take money from the emergency fund that I established to be sure the family is taken care of. It really pierces my heart to see the way the church members uphold him as such a model citizen, one that cares for his family, when he is far from being that person. The members idolize him."

"Wait a minute, sis, this is getting so hard for me to digest right now; how can you continue dealing with this? Sis, I have to applaud you! Ain't no way that I would take such behavior from Stanley, pastor or whatever title he holds!" shouted Gloria. Charlotte continued speaking, fighting to hold back the tears, yet they were escaping from her eyes.

"The only consolation I have is the fact that I will be seeing Fernando on the 17th. The thought of seeing him again fills my heart with such warmth and tenderness. What are your thoughts?"

"Well... Gloria sighed, you know I don't like to get into your personal affairs as I have been understanding with what you are going through with Stanley. I am conflicted about your relationship with Fernando. Have you thought about marital counseling or do you have plans of trying to save your marriage?"

"I have thought about counseling, but at times I think what is the use, since I have suffered so much hurt. The reason that I have stayed this long is for the sake of the children. Akeem will be graduating this year and then there is two years before Jessica will be leaving. If I can only hold on."

"Sis, please don't tell me that you are actually contemplating staying in a *loveless* marriage for two more years and enduring such pain and hurt? What about this preganancy now? Are you going to wait until this child is grown as well?" Gloria stated caringly.

They finally arrived at Gloria's two-story cape cod house located on the other side of the city across the tracks. It seemed that in the construction of major cities a socio-economic separation of living quarters. Sugar enjoyed being in her sister's home on a brisk fall evening where she inhaled the aromotherapy of cinammon and spice candles. The conversation continued between Gloria and Sugar for the majority of the night.

Chapter 5

Charlotte sat at the table quietly as she sipped on a cup of coffee on the 17th... reminiscing about meeting with her true love, Fernando later on that evening. As she was continuing in thought the phone rang and interrupted her process of thought...

"Hello," answered Sugar.

"Hello, baby," whispered Fernando, there was a pause... "Charlotte?"

"Yes," whispered Charlotte. "Fernando, I asked you not to call me on the house phone."

"Yes, Sugar, I know, but I have been calling your cell phone for the past two hours and there hasn't been a response, I was worried and really needed to talk."

"Oh, I dropped my phone in the toilet this morning, had it on the counter and knocked it in the toilet as I was applying my makeup."

"Oh, ok, glad to hear that you are fine; I wanted to tell you that I will be a little late meeting you this evening. I should be there around 7 p.m., got a business meeting that I just couldn't get out of." Fernando sounded relieved.

"Ok, babe, that will be fine, I will see you then," Sugar said.

"Ok, can't wait to see you, my love!" Fernando screamed with excitement. "I love you," he stated passionately.

"I love you too," whispered Sugar.

Wow! That man really does something to me! His voice is very sexy and he possesses the total package. He has so much love that he is willing and able to share with me; there is not a day that goes by that he doesn't prove to me that his love burns deep within for me. What we share is truly divine and special and although it may be difficult for others to understand, I value the love and affection that we share. But at times I do feel conflicted since I am married to a pastor and I serve as the first lady of the church. I also know that God knows my heart and that I genuinely care for this man and how unfulfilled I am in my marriage By his actions my husband has assured me that he doesn't care for me the way he once did. Sometimes when I think of the cruel things he has uttered out of his mouth, I wonder if he ever really truly loved me.

Charlotte looked down at her watch," Oh no, 9:30 a.m. already. I have a meeting at 10:00 a.m., I better get out of here. It's a good thing that I have already selected the clothes that I will wear when I meet Fernando." Charlotte stated to herself. *I know that he loves the pink outfit and the way the pants hug my hips and waist.* Charlotte remembered him saying, *'God really did a number when He created you; you were created with so much love and compassion placed within your heart.' Fernando would often say that my heart has a genuine concern for all people regardless of their titles or status. I must admit that he knows me well and that we connect on so many levels. There is a saying, People come into our lives for a reason, a season, or for a lifetime. I know that Fernando is in it for a lifetime and for the long haul. Although I may be unsure of where my feet will travel and the paths I must cross, I know for certain that whatever the plan God has for me, Fernando will be a part of it.*

Charlotte quickly dialed Gloria while en route to the hotel.

"Hello, Gloria."

"Hey sis, how are you?"

"Wow, what a day! I thought that I would never get out of the office today. It seems that almost everything was working against me today. The meeting was long and it seemed that all of my clients were at the forefront of the discussion today. Today it seems as though the saying, "When it rains, it pours," was scripted for my workday, and my agency possessed the leading role. Today must have been a thunderstorm! I couldn't believe my colleague Bernadette was trying to be the superstar in the meeting today."

"Really sis, how was the drama queen behaving today?"

"She wanted to let everyone know how she was really shining in the executive directors face as though she has all of her clients in check or perhaps she has a magic wand. Bernadette was having her clients line up and walk the straight and narrow! Hell, you would have thought she possessed the secret ingredient for working with clients with mental illnesses. Seemed as though there were no surprises with her clients. I wanted to ask if she had a magic wand she was waving. There is no one who has that much success. Glad that I was able to remain humble and grounded; I don't have to toot my own horn. I keep it real. It is what it is. I know who my source is; Jesus is my provider and this job is only the vehicle!"

"Amen."

"Gloria I know God, said that vengeance is His, but sometimes I want to witness the wrath upon the ones who flaunt things in your face. But this too shall pass!"

"Yes Charlotte, I understand that feeling."

Finally Sugar arrived at the hotel, having feelings of excitement as she prepared for her soulmate to make his entrance. "It has been quite a while since Fernando and I last saw each other; so many things have transpired in the absence of each other. How my heart is waiting to embrace the warmth felt when I see his smiling face. His countenance will certainly add value to my day; what a day it has been with Bernadette flounting around in the Executive Director's face today. One thing is for sure Gloria as the adage states, 'What goes around comes around, and every dog will have its day!' These phrases are words of wisdom as sometimes when others plan for your demise they are surprised when they take the fall instead! Charlotte's sentence came to a screeching halt as Fernando entered the room. Gloria let me call you back later."

For some reason every ounce of frustration that I was feeling just moments ago faded into the background of nothingness and it seems those thoughts happened hours ago.

"Good evening, baby, how was your day?" Fernando asked so sweetly while entering the room.

"My day went well, and yours?" I responded.

I don't want to spoil this moment by filling his head with all of the negative things that transpired in my place of employment. Wow, this man does something to me; it feels as though all of my physical body comes alive and there is so much warmth felt at this time.

He answered, "My day has gone well also."

Fernando came over and greeted Sugar properly by planting a wet passionate kiss softly on her lips. Sugar's juices welled up between the inner parts of her thighs and began to drizzle down her legs. *The lovemaking is awesome between us; it is like our bodies are in complete unison.* Before that thought could complete circling in Sugar's head, Fernando kissed Sugar all over her body and her clothes seemed to peel off her body all at once. Sugar let out a sigh of relief as his manhood entered her temple and filled it with much love. Her body was in sync with his and they rocked back and forth in the sea of lovemaking!

My body has longed for the pleasure this day would bring, and finally it is a reality! My body is responding so positively to this meeting with my lover. Wow, that was intense and welcoming to my body and spirit. I have longed for this touch. It's so refreshing to experience lovemaking for a change instead of experiencing sex, the process of doing it for the sake of fulfilling a need, not because you truly want to or desire to. You know, one of those biological needs?

If I remember correctly, according to Maslow's Hierarchy of Needs, I believe he said sex is one of the basic, foundational, biological or physical needs next to food, shelter and clothing. I could take this a step further and say that Fernando is my sense of balance, bringing everything into perspective or homeostasis. If I go by what Maslow said, Fernando meets the third level as well, which is "belonging and love," the areas of love and affection. According to Maslow, in order for us to reach our greatest potential and become truly motivated, we must continue building, climbing up the pyramid to reach self-actualization. Sugar recognized it is hard to experience love if you lack fulfillment of the most basic need—food. Sugar felt like she had been starving for love and affection with Stanley. *Stanley doesn't know how to touch that secret place and experience the true essence of Me, what lies just beneath the exterior. Fernando is able to peel away and delve into the interior, the innermost part of my being! When I think about it chills go up and down my body; it is rare that one experiences love in this capacity. I thank God for allowing me to experience this type of love.*

Look at Fernando, fast asleep, sleeping like a newborn baby. It hardly ever fails, after a rigorous round of lovemaking, my sweetie quickly drifts off into la la land, the abyss, the spiritual realm of silence and absence from this earthly world as we know it. Sugar speculated, *It is amazing the things that are not known or exposed to us, leaving our cognitions to wonder and attempt to piece the puzzle together. Then there are those of us who have come to the realization that there are things far beyond our understanding and we say, well God knows!*

Well, now I need to process how I am going to tell Fernando what I have been putting off telling him over the phone. I am a woman who likes to face her battles head on. I like to be able to use all of my senses, see the actions of the person, the genuineness of feelings about the discussion, hear the true tone of voice as the discussion proceeds, reflect on the aroma of the place where the discussion transpires, and touch the person during this time, especially when the news may not be favorable. Well, all I can do is tell Fernando what has been on my mind and what I need to share with him.

Just as Sugar continued deep in thought of how she was going to break the news to Fernando, he woke from his nap, turned, looked at and addressed Sugar.

"Hello, beautiful," he stated so warmly.

It is as if whatever he says to me rolls off his lips with such love.

"Hello. Wow honey, I really needed that! I had such a stressful day and now it's like all of the frustration has melted away." Sugar sighed. "Fernando, I don't know where to begin. So much has transpired since we last saw each other; it feels as if an eternity has passed. At least, that's how my heart feels when we are apart for so long."

Fernando responded, "The feeling is mutual. Now, what is it that you need to discuss with me?" His face showed his concern.

"Well, Fernando, I have been doing a great deal of thinking, trying to process where I am at this point in my life. I am in a loveless marriage with two children, I'm the first lady of my church, and a community-based counselor by profession. I have been debating whether or not I want to go back to school for my master's at this stage of my life."

"Sure, Sugar why not?" Fernando stated supportively.

Sugar continued, "The man I truly love is also married. Fernando, will there be room for us in Heaven? I know the Word of God states that He will judge the adulterous; is that who we are?"

As the question departed Sugar's lips, Fernando let out a long sigh and braced himself for what would come next.

Thoughts rushed into his head. *Oh, no,* he wanted to scream, *it can't be that she wants to end the relationship! How can I continue without her? She is one of the few things that I have to look forward to as there are many things in my life that are uncertain at this time—including my marriage. Sugar adds more value to my life than she can imagine.*

Fernando spoke, "Sugar, I don't know how to answer your question. Of course, I want us to both enter into the pearly gates once this life is over. One thing is for certain, there is life after death and death is the beginning of our eternal destination. I am willing to sacrifice whatever I must to be sentenced to life in Heaven. Charlotte, one thing is for certain, when God allowed our paths to cross, he knew how our relationship would unfold. We connect on so many levels, totally and completely. There is so much love that abounds between us. Is it wrong to love? The Word of God also states that our thoughts will never compare to the thoughts of God. There is no way that we will ever understand the way God thinks and the way He has positioned things to be. Let's leave that answer to God and let's be real and true about the genuine love we have for each other."

"Fernando, I knew that you would know what to say that would calm my spirit completely," Sugar stated. "Before we continue in conversation, I first want to tell you how much I love and cherish you," Sugar stated passionately. "There has been a new development since we last spoke; that's what I want to share first."

"Yes?" Fernando uttered.

"I received a call from Dr. Peters' office about a week ago. The nurse was calling to inform me of the results of the routine blood work from my last physical," Sugar continued.

"Ok," Fernando stated as he listened attentively.

"While she was sharing the test results with me she also wanted to be the first to congratulate me. I didn't understand at that moment, until she revealed that when the blood work was collected, it also showed that I am pregnant. I am unsure of how far along I am in the pregnancy; I was instructed to schedule an appointment but I have been in a state of shock and haven't scheduled it yet."

"Oh, wow! That's wonderful!" exclaimed Fernando. "Do you think this is our child?" Fernando stated, smiling. "I have always wanted you to carry my child; I know you will carry her/him with such elegance," Fernando continued.

Sugar took in a deep breath. "Fernando, don't you think this will really complicate matters if I am carrying your child? What about our positions of being married to another? What about my position of being married to a pastor and carrying the title of First Lady?"

"Baby," Fernando said in almost a whisper, "calm down, first of all, take a deep breath. This is a blessing that God has favored you again to prepare your womb for a seed. I am happy and here for you. Charlotte, although this may not be the way that you envisioned this to be, it is a blessing that you could possibly have my baby growing inside of you." He almost squealed with enthusiasm.

Sugar allowed him to continue in discussion without interruption as it was obvious that he needed to vent at this time.

"I have always wanted children and was really shocked when Brenda revealed to me that she didn't want any! I always thought she was being vain when she stated, 'There is no baby worth ruining my figure!' Then she walked over to the full body mirror and stated, 'Well look at me; if it ain't broke don't fix it! I haven't been going to the gym and working out for endless hours for nothing. As a prominent owner of a hair salon and spa there is an image I must uphold.' I thought she was joking at first, until one dreadful day she came home from a doctor's appointment only to tell me that she had just aborted our child! I couldn't believe my ears, when she made the statement so coldly. How could she abort our child, without even alerting me of the existence of the child, or giving me a voice in the decision?

"When that happened approximately five years ago, I almost walked out on her. It was a very depressing time for me. It was at that time that I began talking with my pastor and participating in the church services more. That was what allowed me to make it during that time. When I reflect back to this stage of life, Sugar, I remember that's the one thing that I have not forgiven her for. How could she do such a thing? Is it possible for a marriage to sustain deceit and hidden agendas? I know this is an area that I continue dealing with; although, there hasn't been a great deal of discussion to bring closure to it. When I try talking to her she always makes me feel that I am making such a big deal of the incident. She constantly dismisses the issue. Are my feelings not important?"

Charlotte gasped. "Wow. I had no idea that you were dealing with this, and that the feelings have been this intense and of this magnitude. I know that you have mentioned this to me before, but now that you are explaining it, I really understand the depth of the situation. This must have been and still is a sensitive area, and there is the need for forgiveness so that you will not hold bitterness in your heart, as bitterness has a way of eating away and destroying the essence of your being. I will be praying that God will intervene in this area, especially since it appears that Brenda doesn't feel this matter needs to be addressed."

"Charlotte, thank you," Fernando said. "That's one reason I love you so much; you truly have a compassionate heart and you genuinely care for me."

"Fernando, as for the pregnancy I will be making an appointment next week so that I can be tested and if I am, I will begin the prenatal care immediately. I will be keeping the baby, but establishing the paternity of my unborn child will take care of itself once we schedule the appointment," Charlotte stated empathetically. "This will bring us closure and we will be at peace with the results."

"Charlotte, just rest assured that I am in your corner with whatever the results are; I will always love you no matter what! Now since that is behind us, what is the reason that you initially wanted us to meet?" He sighed, took Sugar's hand and looked directly into her eyes.

"Fernando, I don't know how to begin; I have been carrying this around for what seems like an eternity."

"Sugar, how about starting at the beginning, which is always a good starting point?"

"Ok, but before I begin, Fernando have you ever looked over your life and examined it, feeling that perhaps the reason you are having so many heartaches, disappointments, and mishaps is due to you not doing things according to the way that God intended them to be done?" Sugar questioned hastily.

Fernando looked at Sugar so tenderly before responding, "Sugar, we all at times feel overwhelmed and feel that somehow things have been blocked in our lives and we should have traveled further than we have. I firmly believe that we are exactly where God intends for us to be, and everything that has happened in our lives has been predestined to happen—the good, the bad and the indifferent."

Boy! Fernando, has such intelligence and always knows exactly what to say to silence all doubt in my mind. So this is what true love feels like. Why couldn't I share a love like this with Stanley? That would certainly simplify matters for the both of us.

Sometimes, I ponder over the notion of why I didn't meet Fernando before Stanley and why didn't he meet me before Brenda? At times, it seems that life's journey can be difficult and far beyond our comprehension.

"Fernando, journey with me about six months ago. That was about the climax of the things that were happening in my home and bringing me a great deal of stress. About that time the sisters from the church began coming over to the house taking turns cooking for my husband. This began when he got up in the church and humiliated me, announcing before the congregation that I wasn't performing my wifely duties by not cooking his meals and being at his beck and call, being attentive to him as if I don't work outside the home!"

Fernando put his hands up, motioning for Sugar to stop. "Wait a minute, Sugar, this is a great deal of information that you are giving me to digest! I can't believe that bastard had the audacity to be so insensitive as to suggest before the congregation that you were neglecting your duties as a wife to him. Who the hell does he think he is? Did he not read and comprehend how Christ instructed the husband to show his wife benevolence? Was this his way of showing kindness and compassion to you? Sugar, I am so heated right now I feel like punching him dead in the center of his face! Baby, I am deeply sorry that you had to suffer through all that humiliation! Oh, how I wish I could have been there when this transpired; I bet he wouldn't have tried that again! I would have had a little talk with him. Better yet, I would have commanded that he apologize to you before the congregation; who does he think he is? Who told him that he was in control; who told him that God went on vacation and placed him on the throne?"

"Yes," interjected Charlotte, "those are some of the questions I wanted to have answered; that is one of the reasons that our marriage has been really strained. I couldn't believe what he was doing as he stood there saying those dreadful things in the company of people who don't have my best interest at heart. The church mother even had the nerve to approach me, stating that I should be submissive to him."

"Sugar, there are many people who, due to their insecurities, lack of accomplishments, and

86

frustrations, take any opportunity they can to lash out at someone else so they can feel fulfilled," Fernando stated emphatically. "Let's just move on and not focus on these things any longer as they will only add fuel to the fire that has already been ignited."

"Alright, I don't want to cause you to dwell on this injustice any longer than the time that it is healthy for you to focus on it," stated Sugar. "That brings me to the dilemma that I am presently facing. I have been anticipating leaving my marriage to Stanley; although, I don't know how to approach it. It seems that we are growing farther apart. He is a good father to the children and brings in sufficient income from the church; however, he doesn't provide me with what I really and truly need. It has been difficult for me to move past the treatment and the way that I have been feeling for far too long. Once I decide to leave, I not only have myself to consider but the children as well. I will be leaving for me and not to come running into your arms.

"Fernando, I really love you, but it must be done the right way and I cannot leave him and be seen publicly with you months later. How would that look? Also you should remain with your wife. It is still unclear to me how I will leave him. I am committed to the Lord and the position I have in the church, and if I don't remain a member there I plan to continue staying in my church organizations. I must put away some money so that my family and I will be able to make it without his financial assistance; although, he hasn't been contributing at all to the household finances," Sugar vented.

"Charlotte, you mean Stanley has been withholding monies from you and the children?" questioned Fernando.

"Yes," Sugar answered in almost a whisper. "I didn't mean to add that information; I didn't want to bring up anything that would upset you!"

"Charlotte, just understand that I want the best for you. I am at a crossroads in my relationship/marriage with Brenda as well. She takes me for granted and she has changed drastically since the death of her mother. I did propose to her that we needed counseling in order for our marriage to be sustained. When I presented this notion to her she took it as a joke! There have been years of unhappiness and nonfulfillment between us. Something has to give; I cannot and will not continue living like this! It looks like we both have some soul searching to do. But I feel that the first item on the agenda should be finding out how far along you are in the pregnancy and beginning your prenatal care," Fernando stated with urgency.

Charlotte loved the way he took charge and control with issues that required immediate attention.

"Ok Fernando, I agree that will be the first issue that I address. I feel so relieved that we were able to talk and I was able to get so many issues off of my chest that were bothering me. You know stress can cause physiological problems?"

"Yes, Sugar I am very aware of how stress can affect us adversely; I have experienced it first-hand."

"Now that we have that settled, I am hungry and we need to eat," confessed Sugar.

"Charlotte, I have already taken the liberty of making reservations at our favorite restaurant. I already informed them we would be arriving at 8 p.m."

Following dinner they returned to the room and Sugar was completely amazed when she entered the room and there were red and pink rose petals leaving a walking trail throughout the room that led first to the bathroom where rose petals were floating on top of the water in the Jacuzzi tub.

After they bathed in the tub, Fernando placed his hands over Charlotte's eyes stating, "I have a surprise for you."

What can the surprise be as I have already been greeted by this wonderful surprise? What could top what he has already done?

The rose petals extended into the bedroom and on top of the covers. There were long stem red roses on the table adjacent to the bed accompanied by chocolate-dipped strawberries and a bottle of sparkling white grape juice.

"I would have gotten Champagne, but there is a possibility of you being pregnant."

"Yes, I understand and appreciate you for that." Sugar gleamed.

Sugar looked closely and saw an envelope attached to the roses. When she looked inside, she saw two first-class tickets to Ocho Rios, Jamaica with open ended dates.

Wow, I am in awe, trying to take in this moment. Fernando can be so romantic! To have this arranged while we were out to dinner. I don't believe he's left one stone unturned. I had no idea.

"Fernando, thank you so much for these wonderful gifts. I don't know how I will be able to take this trip, though," Sugar stated anxiously.

"Shhh," Fernando stated in almost a whisper, "don't worry about that for now; I want very much to have some time that we can share together completely with some sense of normalcy. There is a great deal of uncertainty now and that's why the tickets contain open dates. "And... Sugar," he said, looking deeply into her eyes...

The look Fernando is giving me now makes me want to melt.

"You are welcome and you deserve more than money can buy. You are truly invaluable."

At that moment, "A Woman's Worth" by Maxwell, played on the radio. *Talking about sealing a perfect deal; I absolutely love Maxwell! What an awesome experience; we made love throughout the night. Oh, how I love this man! For this time in my life, my journey, I am elated. What we have shared in this time has truly touched the depths of my heart. This is why it's hard for me to leave Fernando; how can you leave someone that shows so much care and compassion? If Stanley showed me an ounce of this affection... well that's wishful thinking! Far from the*

current reality I am facing!

Chapter 6

Brenda entered the salon calling Mr. Perkins, the owner of Perkins Construction via telephone.

"Hello, this is Mrs. Storm, may I speak to Mr. Perkins?"

"Yes dear, you have him; how may I help you?"

"First of all, don't speak to me in that condescending way, I am not your dear, and I don't answer to such a remark!"

"Mrs. Storm, I meant that statement as a term of endearment," Mr. Perkins stated apologetically.

Mr. Perkins continued, "I try to always uplift women, no harm was intended."

"Mr. Perkins, perhaps it's not your job to uplift women; after all, you are a contractor, how about you focus on that field of study?" Brenda stated harshly. "Now, I first want to draw your attention to the tile that you and your ignorant workers laid in the bathroom! The bathroom tiles are the wrong color and they appear differently than the way we discussed and the blueprints of the architectural design! Don't think that because you are conducting business with a woman that you don't need to put your best foot forward! You are not dealing with an ignorant or a passive woman! I expect you to meet me in my office in the next five minutes so that we can be sure that we are on the same page concerning these renovations! If you are unable or ill-equipped to perform the job, I don't mind consulting one of your competitors!" She hung up the phone.

While Brenda waited in her office for Mr. Perkins to come, her anger intensified regarding the lack of professionalism, organization, and prestige of his construction company.

How could I have been such a fool as to hire such an incompetent bunch?

Brenda's thought was interrupted when she heard a loud boom, crash, crash! Brenda ran out of her office to find herself ducking as a huge boulder flew over her head and crashed into the adjoining wall. Brenda could hardly believe her eyes and she witnessed holes as big as coasters in the wall as she tried to discern what just happened.

Mr. Perkins ran over to provide assistance to Brenda to ensure that she was in the arc of safety.

"Brenda, are you okay?" Mr. Perkins questioned.

"What kind of stupid question is that? Of course I'm not okay, due to the negligence of your company, I have twisted my ankle as I tried to dodge that big boulder!" Brenda responded, exasperated. "Please remove yourself and your company from my premises! You will be hearing from my lawyer!" Brenda yelled.

"Sally," Brenda called, "do you mind calling my doctor's office to see if I can be worked in today? I don't want to take a trip to the emergency room as it is likely crowded and there will be no telling what time I will make it out."

Sally pondered concerning Brenda's mannerisms, 'Do I mind?' Sally noticed the only time Brenda spoke to her decently was when it was to her benefit. Sally comprehended if Brenda could speak to her adequately now, she could always speak to her in a like manner.

Sally responded, "Sure," as Brenda interrupted her thoughts.

Sally realized the only reason she continued working there was to ensure she would be able to pay her way through school, and although Brenda didn't have a good attitude, she was paid well and had some autonomy in her work.

"Brenda, they can work you in if you are able to come now," Sally reported.

"Sally, do you mind taking me to this appointment? If you are there over your scheduled time to be off, I will pay you double time."

"Sure, Brenda let me call my childcare provider to alert her that I will be picking up the children late due to having this emergency situation to address, as Al is working late tonight."

Life is funny, a person should never kick or mistreat a person as they are ascending up, for they never know when they will have to be sweet or kind to them when they approach a tough spot. You never know when you have to depend on others. Sally reflected on the times she sacrificed her time away from her family for Brenda on several occasions and Brenda continued expressing no appreciation for the sacrifice of her precious time. Sally pondered, *I am beginning to think that maybe I am the fool to continue being available at her beck and call.* "Brenda, allow me to move my car to the entrance of the building so you won't have to walk so far to get to the car," she stated compassionately. Sally embraced only being responsible for the way she treated people not the way people treated her. She believed sometimes it was hard living by biblical principles when being mistreated.

Brenda hobbled her way into the entrance of her house, being careful not to topple over, manipulating the crutches into the foyer where she caught a glimpse of the chandelier that had spiderwebs cascading down like icicles draping from the rooftop at the end of a snowy night.

Brenda stated under her breath, "Boy, I really do need to clean up around here before the dust and dirt take the house over completely. Or better yet, I need to advertise a position available here for a maid or to be politically correct, an "environmental specialist," since cleaning is so beneath me! How am I going to rest for the next two weeks? The better question would be how am I going to finagle my way around this house with these crutches? I have so much on my plate, but if I don't do it myself it will not get done. I have a bunch of incompetent workers at the salon so there is no way that I can be here and still oversee what is happening there.

"Brenda, is that you?" a deep scratchy voice descended down from the upstairs bedroom.

Brenda cognitively addressed the following questions: Who else would be opening the door with the key? Are you serious, Fernando? Brenda knew she needed to be mindful that she may need his assistance during this time. Many thoughts rushed through Brenda's mind at once, but she felt it better to entertain his asinine question.

"Yes, it's me, honey," she stated bluntly.

"Brenda, where have you been? I have been worried," he stated emphatically while coming down the stairs to meet her in the foyer.

"What happened?" he questioned when he saw the crutches.

"I had an accident in the salon with the incompetent construction company that I hired to complete the renovations at Beautiful Diva's," Brenda continued. "You would think that when you have been quoted a price of $60,000 for renovations, the company performing them would be competent. But I guess we can't put our complete confidence in a price, right?"

"Yes, that is a valid point, dear, Exactly when did the accident happen?"

"Well, it happened around 3 o'clock this afternoon. Sally was able to secure and transport me to an appointment at my primary care physician's office to spare me the agony of sitting in the emergency room for hours!"

"Getting back to the subject at hand, why am I just being made aware of this accident as it happened several hours ago."

Brenda took in a deep breath.

"Well, Fernando, I didn't want to worry you as I knew you had just returned from your business conference and I knew you would be very tired."

Brenda knew that she must handle Fernando circumspectly as he would be essential to her recovery.

"Brenda, although I may be tired, I want to know that you are safe and everything is well with you. I don't want you to feel the need to keep information from me just because I'm tired. I will always make myself available for you. So how long will you be out of work?" Fernando stated compassionately.

"Well, my physician says that I will be out for the next six weeks; that will be the length of time it will take for the bones to fuse back together. I don't know how I'm going to manage being out of work for that long. Of course I'm not concerned with the money as I am always prepared for that—I have plenty in my emergency savings. I'm going to have to check on my employees as they are not as competent as I would like—"

Fernando interrupted, "What about Sally? She seems to always be attentive to your and the business's needs. Isn't she the one who took you to the doctor to ensure that your medical needs were being met?"

"Well, yes, but just because someone takes you to the doctor, answers calls, makes calls, and schedules appointments, doesn't mean they are competent to run the office in my absence," she said matter of factly.

"Brenda, have you given Sally a chance or did you just arrive at that conclusion? I was just trying to offer a recommendation for your consideration."

"If I wanted your opinion, Fernando, I would have asked or offered what an acceptable opinion would be!"

"I was wondering when the true Brenda would re-surface! Why does it always have to be the way you envision it to be?" Fernando questioned sincerely.

"Tell me how many times have you worked in the salon with me? In the ten years that I have been in business you have been there on five different occasions assisting me with some of the projects. You may have seen Sally do some things around the office, but I am not about to give her any more power than she already possesses! You must be out of your ever-loving mind if that is your process of thought! I will continue going into *my* business every day and that settles it!"

Brenda's anger intensified. Fernando excused himself from the room.

Fernando prayed earnestly, "How long, oh God, will I be able to endure living here with Brenda? Is this all that marriage has to offer? Has this marriage run its course? Was it the right decision when I decided she was the woman that I couldn't do without? Is this marital relationship worth salvaging? Please give me the wisdom and understanding to discern the best path to take on this present journey. Amen."

Fernando entered the room once again where Brenda was.

"Brenda, we need to talk."

"About what?" Brenda scoffed.

"Please, let's sit over here on the couch so that we can discuss it with a clear mind."

"Ok," Brenda agreed.

"Brenda, there are some things that I must discuss with you. First of all, for many years now I have felt that you don't consider my thoughts and feelings. It appears most of the time when we are engaged in conversation it has to flow on your terms. If things are not going your way, then you want to quickly bring the conversation to a screeching halt! Why is that? Do you feel you have all the answers? I have allowed you to have your space, especially since much of this treatment began when your mother passed away."

"Oh boy, Fernando, here we go! I don't feel that I have all the answers, but it appears that in many of the conversations I entertain, I am the one possessing the most knowledge."

"See, that's what I'm talking about right there; you always come across as being sarcastic in your responses. I am really tired of this. It's time for us to make a decision; do we want to continue in this marriage? Are you willing for us to participate in marriage counseling? There are so many things that need to be addressed and I think that we need some professional intervention."

"*You* think? Do I have a say in this decision or am I to hop on it because you think it's a bright idea?" Brenda scolded.

"Yes, I feel that it will give resolution and shed light on a lot of our issues. I understand that Ms.

Nelly is licensed and provides counseling for married couples that have marital issues requiring discussion or repair. You do still love me, don't you?"

"Of course I love you, Fernando, but I have been feeling alienated from you and everyone since my mother passed away."

"Brenda, what do you mean you have been feeling alienated? You have been alienating yourself from me and everyone else. Everytime I want to have some dialogue, it seems that you always find a way to excuse yourself or you begin an argument," Fernando stated matter of factly.

"Fernando! That's not the way it is; you always want to monopolize the conversation, shedding light on the issues you feel that I need to come up in. 'Brenda, you are doing this, Brenda you are doing that.' Whine, Whine, Whine. Being the victim in each conversational exchange! The truth is I don't have to do a damn thing that you or anyone else requests of me!" Brenda yelled. "Now, Fernando I am through with this!"

"Brenda, this is my final plea; if we don't receive some marriage counseling or some type of professional intervention, I don't know if there is hope," Fernando stated with much compassion. "Look at us! You have just sustained an injury and we are not able to be at peace even during a time of storm. We need some intervention, Brenda!" Fernando pleaded.

"Well, I am surprised that you didn't say that God would work it out. It seems that in situations like this you and everyone else seems to throw Him into the mix," Brenda verbalized sarcastically.

"Brenda, I am through with it." Throwing his hands up in mid air.

Chapter 7

Sugar took in a deep breath when she entered Dr. Peters' office.

What am I doing here at this stage of my life? I have a child about to finish high school and another who will graduate in the next two years. I am over 40 years old, in my prime stage of life and very much anticipating shifting some baggage out of my life. Now, I am about to begin again... wow. Perhaps I should have made an appointment with a shrink instead.

Sugar was processed in by the receptionist, was seated, and waited for her name to be called by the nurse. She scanned the waiting room, dissecting the demographics of the clientele. There were two couples in conversation, preparing for the new addition to their family; three women were seated alone.

I wonder what their stories are? Everyone has a story to tell. My story isn't one that I'm too proud of. Still trying to figure out whose baby I'm carrying. Is this the right time to leave my marriage? At least right now I have some form of stability.

Suddenly Nurse Kelly appeared directly in front of Sugar, waving her hands.

"Mrs. Spickley, I have been calling you for about five minutes now."

"Really?" Sugar questioned shamefully. "I must have been in deep thought," she stated.

"That's very apparent, guess you are still trying to get over the shock." Nurse Kelly chuckled.

"That's an understatement! Akeem is about to graduate high school and preparing to enter college while Jessica will be graduating in two more years! Now I'm at the point of starting over. How do you think you would feel being in my situation? You don't know what people face until you have to travel in their shoes. I don't think it's a laughing matter This really concerns me... it appears you are being insensitive!" Sugar's tone of voice intensified.

"Charlotte, please calm down, I apologize. I didn't mean any harm; I was trying to help you to relax. Laughter is good medicine," Kelly stated compassionately.

"Well, it felt like an attack against me!" Sugar stated. "Laughter is good medicine when the topic is mutual and agreeable."

"Again, Charlotte, I apologize and I will try not to be insensitive to you in your situation."

"Thanks Kelly, let's just move on with the visit, shall we?"

I don't feel like discussing this anymore. I have other things to devote my time and energy to. After all, I have made my point. Ok, I have been waiting here for about 30 minutes, where is Dr. Peters? It doesn't take but a few minutes for me to disrobe.

As this thought was completing…

Dr. Peters entered the exam room.

"Well hello, Mrs. Spickley, how are you feeling this morning?"

"Doctor, I have seen better days."

"Are you feeling under the weather?" Dr. Peters questioned.

"No, I'm speaking of the fact that I am at the point of starting over again."

"Well, have you considered your options? You can have an abortion, or give the child up for adoption. There are many people who would love to welcome a new baby into their home."

Sugar gasped. "Dr. Peters... I am a woman of faith and would never consider aborting my child! And there is no way that I would consider giving my baby up for adoption. I could never have another child that I am unable to see, hold and love; it was detrimental when I was forced to give my daughter up for adoption many years ago. It still pains me when I think or talk about it. Almost drove me to an early grave, but what options did I have? My parents were against the rearing of a baby ruining my life. I can still hear them clearly state, 'You are going to college and going to make something out of your life!' they screamed in harmony. I'm still haunted by those memories.

"I can remember so vividly the day that the nurse came in and told me she had handed my daughter over to the Department of Social Services and there was a family waiting to adopt her. I still have the booties that she wore while in the hospital. I just wept! I cried for the next month. My mother would come into my room, and practically shove food down my throat. I had no appetite. Now as I reflect back, I know I was going through depression; wow, that was truly an adjustment. Thank you for listening, Dr. Peters, I have been holding this in for far too long."

"You are welcome, Charlotte, in this profession I realize that sometimes it's beneficial to lend a listening ear," Dr. Peters stated empathetically. "Although, this may be a late stage in life, I believe that this has surfaced for a reason. Alright then, shall we proceed to the exam?" questioned Dr. Peters.

"Certainly, that's why I am here."

Although I know that being a gynecologist is a legitimate career I often wonder while I'm being examined if the physician is ever excited by any of their patients. I will be glad when I am out of here. Coming to the GYN is among the last places I would choose to be.

"Ok, Mrs. Spickley I have completed your exam; you are eight weeks pregnant. I have written out your prenatal vitamin prescriptions. Which pharmacy would you like me to send them to?"

"You can send them to Walgreens. Dr. Peters, you are bound by the laws of confidentiality, correct?"

"Of course, is there something on your mind?"

"Yes, I have been having an affair and I am unsure if this child is the product of my affair or not. Don't misunderstand me, it's not a casual affair; I don't believe in those. I love him very much and I am having some marital problems."

"I understand completely. Shall I perform a paternity test for you?" Dr. Peters inquired.

"Yes, I think that should be the next step. Are there any risks involved to my unborn child?"

"The test can be performed with miminal risk, it is called a Non-Invasive Prenatal Paternity or NIPP, which entails analyzing and preserving the baby's DNA naturally found in your bloodstream. It will be a simple collection of your blood."

"Ok, thank you, Dr. Peters, I just don't know how to proceed if my lover is the father. I do understand that this was the risk of having unprotected intercourse. I will call the office to schedule the test."

"Very well, Mrs. Spickley."

Whew, finally that task is over! But I'm still not out of the woods yet. There are still some things that have to be decided. Mama used to say, "Sugar, if you lay down with dogs you gonna get up with fleas!" That was to say that whatever decision we make there's always a consequence. I am happy that I could possibly be carrying his child; after all, I love him dearly. I do have mixed feelings as I am married to another, have children, and a ministry is involved.

Based on the way I have been scolded before, I can imagine what the "sisters" will have to say concerning this "juicy news." It will spread like a forest fire in the heart of summer. The flames will be unquenchable. "For the power of life and death lies in the tongue." Many people commit murder of their brothers and sisters with the stroke of the tongue! It's amazing how bad news travels quickly, but good news travels like a snail.

Almost audibly... "Wow, I am really in a pickle. Where did I park my car? The staff here are forever stating their policy is 'to cater to the needs of our patients,' really? If that were true they would invest in valet parking so you wouldn't have to walk a mile to your vehicle. That is truly a stretch for me in my condition.

Charlotte traveled home frantically fumbling through her purse trying to locate her phone. *Where is my phone? I placed it in the same outside flat pocket so I could easily access it! Doggit, I must have left my phone in the doctor's office. I can't believe this!*

Charlotte contemplated, *There are so many things positioning themselves against me at this moment! Well, there is no other choice but to go back to Dr. Peters' office and retrieve it.* Finally, Charlotte felt relieved as she left the doctor's office and traveled back toward her house.

She wondered if Fernando was available. *Well, there's only one way to find out.*

"Hello, Fernando."

"Hello, my love," he stated with such warmth and compassion. "How are you doing?"

"Well. Fernando, I am just leaving Dr. Peters' office. He examined me and I am indeed pregnant."

"Yayyy!" Fernando squealed with excitement. "How far along are you, sweetie?" questioned Fernando.

"I'm eight weeks or two months pregnant," Charlotte responded in almost a whisper.

"Baby," replied Fernando, "you don't sound as if you are happy that this child was made out of love between the both of us."

"Fernando, it's not that. While meeting with Dr. Peters there were some things that were unearthed that I thought I had worked through. When we began talking, those feelings came rushing back at once and I realized that there is still a void. The other issue is we must establish the paternity of the baby; it is a possibility that it could be Stanley's."

"Wait a minute, Charlotte. What was 'unearthed' that you felt you had worked through?"

"Fernando, I cannot discuss that right now. I don't have the energy or strength. I just want to go home, take a warm bath and lie down. This has been a very exhausting day. I need to concentrate on my driving anyway; they are doing construction on this highway again. Every time I turn around there is construction, some alterations to the land. Building up and tearing down, my grandfather stated those were the signs of the end of times! Oh, no what is this, a detour? I didn't see a sign."

"A sign?" questioned Fernando intensely waiting for a response. "Charlotte, what's happening? Charlotte?"

Oh, God what has happened? Let me try her phone... Ring, ring. "You have reached the voicemail of Charlotte Spickley, please leave a message and I will return your call as soon as possible. Make this a great day!"

"Charlotte, dear, your call was lost. Please return my call as soon as you can. I'm worried!"

Fernando tried Sugar's phone again... ring, ring... the call went straight to voicemail.

What could have happened? The last thing discussed was construction and a detour on the interstate. Which interstate could she have taken? She was leaving Dr. Peters' office.

Chapter 8

Fernando jumped into his car and traveled to Interstate 9 in record time, he moved with a sense of urgency! As Fernando approached the construction site, it was surrounded by blue lights and an ambulance was on the scene as well. Traffic was at a standstill.

Thank God I have my EMT credentials, and am able to break through this traffic. My heart almost stopped when I saw the tail end of Sugar's car.

"Oh, Lord please let Charlotte and the baby be okay. Please Lord, please."

That's all Fernando could utter as he moved closer. The paramedics were there and had already used the heavy artillery to cut her out of the car. "Oh, God please let her be okay."

"Hello, you guys need any assistance? How is the individual?"

Mark, one of the paramedics responded, "She has suffered a concussion, and we're unsure of the condition of her spine. We were careful removing her. We will be transferring her to the hospital."

"Okay, I will follow you then."

"Fernando, you know her?"

"Yes, Mark she is a very close, dear friend of mine."

"Ok, I understand," Mark stated empathetically.

Fernando jumped in his car, placed the red siren on the outside of the car and followed the ambulance full speed. Fernando continued uttering prayers up to God as he was driving to the hospital. Fernando arrived at the emergency room.

"Fernando, Charlotte will be going straight into surgery," Mark stated with urgency.

"Great, that's wonderful. I'm glad emergency surgery will be performed. I want all to be well with her. Please let the surgeon know I will be in the waiting room."

Fernando prayed, "Lord, God please bless Charlotte through the surgery, please guide the hands of the surgeon, and please allow her to return to optimal health. Lord, God let me be satisfied with the outcome, realizing that you do all things well! Thank-you, God. I bless your name for this blessing in Jesus' name."

Fernando rushed up to the second level of the hospital to the surgical waiting area. Fernando had been waiting about 30 minutes when Gloria entered the waiting area.

"Hello Fernando, how are you?" Gloria hugged him tightly.

"I am so happy to see you, well… not under these circumstances. I have been a wreck, unsure of what is happening. She has been in surgery for the past 30 minutes, don't know how extensive it is at this time," Fernando stated in almost a whisper.

"I can't understand. What happened, Fernando? Of course she had me listed as the next of kin along with Stanley so I was contacted and made aware there had been a car accident."

"Well, Gloria, I was on the phone talking with her after she left the doctor's office and she was sharing the results. She did sound a bit distraught, and as we continued talking she stated there was some construction on the interstate. I quickly rushed to I-9 and saw the back end of her car. She hit the ditch and the edge of a tree. Gloria, the paramedics and EMTs had to cut her out. I arrived in time to see her on the stretcher, but she was in critical condition. Mark, the paramedic on the scene, informed me they were careful moving her since they weren't sure of the injuries she sustained. If they called you at the same time they called Stanley, where is he?"

"Well, Fernando, I'm sure that you have heard about his character!"

Gloria was forced to end her statement as they witnessed Stanley passing the waiting room, with five large pizzas in tow. Gloria, puzzled by what she witnessed, questioned Stanley concerning the pizzas.

"Stanley, what the hell are you doing bringing pizzas here?"

"First of all, Gloria, watch your tone! You will not speak to me in just any way!"

Gloria rose from her seat. "Let's understand something, this is not Sugar standing here; I have no problem putting you in your place!"

"Gloria, I don't have time for your shenanigans! I have to get this to these hungry people!" Stanley stated matter-of-factly

"You mean to tell me you had the audacity to stop off and get pizza and you don't know your wife's status?" Gloria stated with much disappointment.

"Gloria, Gloria I don't have time for this! I need to deliver this pizza before it gets cold; please, excuse me, and move out of my way," Stanley stated with much agitation.

"So, the delivery of the pizza is more important than the update on your wife?"

"It's important that I deliver these pizzas to the staff that have been taking care of my wife! For your information I have already received an update on her condition! Now, if I may be excused..." and he proceeded to walk away.

"Fernando, can you believe that jackass? How can he be so insensitive?" she said fighting back tears that were escaping from her eyes.

"Gloria, please calm down," he stated as he embraced her. Fernando held Gloria in his arms, and she burst into tears.

Gloria mused, *No wonder Charlotte is able to love Fernando; he has a very gentle soul.* Gloria gathered he had no problem showing his compassion without feeling that he wasn't a man. He showed it is possible for a man to be in touch with his emotional side and remain a man. She wished for Sugar's sake that Stanley was able to realize that. Gloria really struggled with respecting Stanley and viewing him as a man of the cloth. There used to be a time when people could say that God called them into the ministry and it wouldn't be questioned and people would yield to them and would give them anything they requested. Those days have long passed and people are not only listening to sermons, but watching the ministers' lives as well.

"Fernando, thanks for understanding the emotional breakdown, I just don't know what Stanley is thinking! How can he be so insensitive during this time? My sister is in a very critical state right now and we don't know what condition she will be in after it is over. Fernando, can we please pray right now? I need a touch from God."

"Sure, Gloria, I would be happy to do that." Gloria and Fernando bowed their heads for prayer. Stanley burst in the door, failing to excuse himself.

"Gloria, can I speak to you for a moment? We need to talk."

Gloria took in deep breaths of air.

"Stanley, I don't think this is a good time," Fernando interrupted. "Do you understand we were about to pray when you entered the room?"

"Who are you?" Stanley questioned in a rude tone.

"I am a friend of Gloria's and Charlotte's. Please let us have a moment," Fernando stated politely.

"I was just asking to speak with Gloria and I don't understand what the big problem is!" Stanley stated, sounding irritated.

"Stanley, please leave now," Fernando stated.

"The last time I checked this was a public place with a sign posted out front reading East Side Regional Medical Center, accessible to those who are here for loved ones having surgery, but I will be the better person and leave this place," Stanley stated harshly.

"Whew." Gloria blew out a long breath. "What a relief. I thought he would never leave. Now Fernando, will you please lead us in prayer? I greatly need God's intervention."

"Gladly," stated Fernando. "Father God, in the precious name of Jesus, we come to You as humbly as we can, first and foremost we ask that you would forgive us for all the sins we have committed, both known and unknown; we repent of them at this very moment. We praise you for your supreme authority as the King of Kings and the Lord of Lords! Thank you for all that you are to us! We touch and agree on the behalf of your dear daughter, Charlotte! Lord, we ask you to continue guiding the hands of the surgeon at this moment, be with her and comfort her through the surgery, through the pain. We thank you in advance, realizing you are Jehovah Rapha, the God that heals and we ask for your divine healing! We ask that you would command all of her internal organs to function the way they should! We ask you to uphold us during this time. We ask these things in the precious name of Jesus! Amen."

"Amen," Gloria chimed in. "Fernando, I really thank you for that beautiful prayer that you ushered up! I do feel better. I really hate that scene with Stanley, but I just don't understand him."

Stanley captured Gloria and Fernando's attention and they turned their heads in unison as he entered the room escorting a young lady in a skin tight red dress under a white three quarter length leather coat.

From the looks of things, she meets Sugar's description of Sister Candy, Gloria made an internal evaluation.

"Gloria, Fernando, this is Sister Candy Willoughby from the church; she wanted to come and see about First Lady Spickley."

"Hello," stated Fernando and Gloria in unison.

Time passed, family members, friends, and church members arrived.

Gloria was not thrilled with her current reality of sharing such close quarters with people whom she was not interested in being with for hours. It was beginning to really frustrate and unnerve her, especially considering the disagreement she'd had with Stanley. Gloria uttered in an undertone, "This too shall pass! It will not be long before this memory will be behind me."

"Good evening, I am the surgeon, Dr. Turner and this is Nurse Jennifer Adams. We need to speak with the Spickley family concerning your loved one," Dr. Turner requested earnestly.

In response to the request, about 20 people rose from their seats simultaneously.

"This meeting needs to be conducted with close family and friends whose names Mr. Spickley has provided to our staff."

"Jesus, keep me near the cross," mumbled Gloria under her breath.

Gloria dwelled on the audacity of Stanley providing a list of people that he felt should be included in the conversation concerning the health of her sister! She felt he should have included their Mama and her in that decision, or at the very least, he should have involved their mother in deciding who to share such sensitive information with.

"Could I get the following people to follow me into the conference room: Candy Willoughby, Gloria Pettaway, Doreen Cantaloupe...?"

"Just as I thought," Gloria mumbled under her breath, "Stanley placed Candy's name first on the list and had Mom and me positioned on the list after her like we are Sugar's friends and Candy is her family."

Gloria moved over and stood beside Stanley, careful not to cause a scene.

"Stanley, will you please have Fernando added to the list? He is a friend of mine and I would like him present," Gloria requested.

"What is Fernando's last name?" Stanley queried.

"It's Sexton," Gloria responded.

Stanley approached the doctor with urgency. "Excuse me, Dr. Turner, would you be so kind as to add Fernando Sexton to the list?" Stanley requested.

"Sure, Fernando Sexton please join the group," insisted Dr. Turner. "You come highly recommended."

Gloria prayed quietly, "Father God, in the matchless name of Jesus, please equip me with the strength to endure whatever information the doctor will be releasing concerning the health of my sister. Please God, don't let my natural fleshly feelings get in the way of what's being done in the spiritual realm. Please forgive me for all of my sins committed and accept this prayer from a true living vessel. Thank you in advance for your richness and bountiful blessings. In Jesus' name. Amen."

Dr. Turner began speaking, "I was the surgeon operating on Charlotte and I wanted to provide you with an update concerning her condition. I would first like to start by saying that she is stable, but her situation is critical. She lost a great deal of blood and she required a blood transfusion, she received two pints of blood. Due to her striking the tree on the driver's side of the car, she sustained injury to her lower vertebrae, spine, and coccyx. The surgery was very successful; however, we are not sure if she will ever walk again. When she awakened from the surgery an assessment was performed and it was discovered she has paralysis in her lower extremities."

Gloria gasped, "Oh no. Dr. Turner, what exactly does that mean?"

"It was determined there is no feeling in the lower half of her body," Dr. Turner replied. Dr. Turner continued, "She has a Foley catheter. Although she sustained this type of injury, the fetus remains intact and is doing fine."

"Huh, fetus?" Stanley asked, almost in a daze.

"Yes Stanley, by our determination she is about eight weeks pregnant. You will soon be welcoming another addition to the family."

Stanley mustered a smile.

Stanley wondered why he had to find out his wife was carrying a baby in the company of their family and friends. Stanley was having a few mixed feelings about having another child at this point in his life. Why didn't Sugar come to him? Sugar must have suspected she was pregnant. Her 28-day cycle was like clockwork; however, he had been preoccupied lately and not concentrating on her cycle. Stanley reflected back on the fact they always knew when she was pregnant with both of their children.

Stanley quietly stated, "I am going to have to have a heart to heart talk with her. I will get to the bottom of this."

Dr. Turner opened the floor for questions. "When will we be able to see her?" questioned Doreen.

"Well, you can go in immediately to see her, but she has had a long day and needs her rest. It is our recommendation that you all spend no more than three hours here. She has a great deal of healing to reach her optimal health. At this time, I am unsure of what that picture will look like," Dr. Turner verbalized.

Doreen quickly intervened proudly, "Dr. Turner, we are people of faith and we believe that God has the final say. You have given your report and now we will wait to hear what our Father's report will be."

To their surprise, Dr. Turner said, "May God be with you."

Cousin Gladys turned to Cousin Sylvia. "Girl, did you see Stanley's face when he questioned the doctor's report of the fetus?"

"Yes, girl I detected a great element of surprise. Looks like something is going on. Sylvia, I smell a big, fat rat."

Doreen headed down the hall to the room to visit with her daughter, Sugar. *I can hardly wait to visit with my daughter again, to gaze into her eyes, to behold the beauty that she possesses.* Doreen believed that God would heal Sugar in record time and that she would testify and proclaim the miracle of living life wholly. Doreen was reminded of the scripture, "The power of life and death lies in the tongue" (Proverbs 18:21). She professed, "We have the choice of speaking positive or negative things into the lives of our loved ones. Through our choice of words, the spiritual realm is orchestrated and brought into alignment. I choose to speak life."

Doreen appeared a bit somber as she approached the entrance to the room of her child, her oldest daughter.

Doreen remembered how fragile Sugar was at the tender age of 15 as she laid in the hospital bed after she delivered her first child. Doreen knew it was impossible to travel back in time, but she wished she hadn't allowed her husband to influence her to pressure their daughter into giving their first grandchild up for adoption. She knew now it was a very devastating time and event for Sugar to live through. Looking back on that event, Doreen realized now that it has been a thorn in their relationship. Doreen reflected on how much their relationship had shifted, even more than expected, after that event. She pondered how she told her daughter it would be alright and she had never experienced anything close to being forced to give her child up for adoption.

"How could I have been so insensitive to her needs?"

"Father God, I ask you to give me the words to utter to my daughter to heal our relationship completely. I ask that you orchestrate the time for us to speak candidly concerning our feelings toward the events that have happened throughout our lives. Thank you, God; I count it done in Jesus' name."

"Good evening, my dear princess. How are you?" Doreen smiled warmly as she entered Charlotte's room.

Princess? It has been years since I heard my mother refer to me as her princess, Sugar thought.

"Hi Mom, I am doing well. Having a little pain, but all is well. For some reason I am not able to feel my lower extremities; it feels like they are not part of my body. They feel heavy as lead; perhaps it's a result of the surgery and the medication I am under," Charlotte stated groggily. "Mom, it sure feels good to hear you refer to me as princess again." Charlotte smiled.

"Yes, Sugar sometimes when things are uncertain with our loved ones, our eyes are opened and we realize that there are some wrongs we need to right. I am by no means elated concerning the accident that landed you in this hospital. I thank God that it wasn't worse. I could be preparing to put my daughter in a grave! Thank you, God! You have granted me time to spend with my daughter! Sugar, I would like to ask for your forgiveness for demanding that you give your daughter, your first born, away for adoption. I didn't understand the agony it caused you at the time. It was more important to your father and me what the family and community would think of us. We didn't consider the impact on you, losing your first child. Will you forgive me?" requested Doreen with much compassion.

"Mom, I know our relationship has been very rocky, and yes I have been sowing seeds of bitterness toward you, and moving past the event, I have had a difficult time forgiving you for depriving me of being a mother to my first-born child. It has been a struggle, watching little girls in the neighborhood, aching inside, wanting to know the whereabouts of my child. There has not been a single day that has passed that I don't think of her. Every year I celebrate her birthday, mostly inside and with tears. Occasionally, I have gone to a restaurant, ordered food and a birthday sundae, which is very painful. Akeem and Jessica don't know she exists! How do you feel knowing that you have another grandchild out there? Mom, does it bother yo—?"

Doreen interrupted, "My dear Sugar, at the time this was happening I didn't understand the full extent of what was taking place. I didn't understand the consequences of my and your father's actions while it was unfolding."

Sugar didn't give consideration to her mother's statement; it appeared she turned a deaf ear to her mother, sighed, and continued.

"Do you really understand the magnitude of pain that event caused? Mom, I have been trying to understand how you and Dad could come together and convince me that giving my baby away was the only way to salvage our family's image. It still rings in my ear like a church bell rang in the old days to signal it was time for service, what you and Daddy said to me in harmony, 'What would the pastor and the congregation say/do if they were to find out that one of the associate ministers of the church's daughter is pregnant out of wedlock? How can we continue standing on the Word of God and our daughter has committed sin privately and as a punishment for the sin of fornication; the production of a baby!'

Those words were so cold! There was never any consideration of how I was impregnated. There was no consideration that I loved Bobby and he was my first and this was the way that he stated our love would be proven. Well, I guess Bobby proved his love by walking out of my life, once he was given the ultimatum that he would have to marry me in order for the child to be kept. He didn't feel that he was ready for that responsibility at age 17. So Mom, is the baby the sin? The product of the sin, fornication? She was conceived in love."

Doreen nodded her head in agreement, "Yes."

"I was sent to Pennsylvania to live with my Aunt Nancy and Uncle Bill until my baby's birth. At that stage in my life when I needed to be surrounded by close family and friends, I was with your sister and her husband. Not to say they are not family, but I felt that I was a disappointment. How could I alert my friends to what I was dealing with? I had to secretly deal with it. I just thank God that I was able to speak with Gloria once she was a little older, but at the time I was dealing with the grief, there was no one to share it with.

"Do you realize I was constantly reminded of the sin I committed when making this child? It has not been an easy journey. I have been suffering in silence; as I was banned from sharing this secret with anyone. I wanted to keep my child; however, my wants were not taken into consideration at all! This is so paramount now that I almost lost my life in the car

153

accident. Mom, I want my daughter in my life and I want her to know her siblings and that I never wanted to give her away. I don't know what she is thinking of me at this time. I don't know who had the pleasure of rearing her. It is a mystery what she has been dealing with in the absence of her biological moth—"

"Alright Sugar," Doreen interrupted politely, "I have patiently listened to you going on and on for the past hour. Now, I want you to rest, as you have endured much stress associated with the accident. I understand now that you have expounded on your experiences, just how much of a mistake I made by not intervening when your father made his request known. Concerning the adoption information, we can begin at Montgomery Department of Family Services.

"Now that I finally have your attention," Doreen continued, "I would like to apologize for assisting your father in forcing you to give up your child, my grandchild. At the time I thought it was for the best and the only way to deal with the issue at the time. Sugar, you were not in a position to raise a child; for heaven's sake, you were 15 at the time. Your father and I didn't want your life and potential to be shattered by raising a child. My dear Sugar, it was not my intention to hurt you or to bring so many agonizing years concerning the absence of your daughter into your life. Please accept my apology," she pleaded. "After you have healed physically I will assist you in searching for your daughter," Doreen stated sympathetically.

"Ok, Mom I will forgive you, but I refuse to forget the turmoil that this has caused me all these years," Sugar stated affirmatively.

Chapter 9

Doreen opened her mouth in response to Charlotte's statement, but in burst Stanley.

"Ms. Doreen, how long do you anticipate being in here? There are others of us, who wish to visit with Sugar!" Stanley stated egotistically.

Doreen responded quickly, "Stanley, I have been visiting with my daughter, as she has undergone much stress and anguish, and we are blessed that she is still with us. I discern you have not been the best husband for my daughter or son-in-law to me for that matter. You will not enter into this room where there is peace and tranquility and upset the normal flow! I will not allow you to mistreat my daughter on my watch! I perceive that you have taken the liberty of mistreating my daughter and you are continuing this behavior even at a time when she desperately requires your assistance with the medical issues she is currently battling! Stanley, doesn't Christ teach you to show your wife benevolence? Is the treatment you are extending to my daughter reflective of such love and compassion? So with that being said you may wait in the hallway until I have completed the time that I desire to spend with my daughter!"

Sugar lifted her head and looked Doreen directly in the eyes for the first time since Doreen had been in her presence today and stated, "Thanks, Mom! I appreciate you taking that stand for me. I don't have the energy to deal with him or that behavior right now. I saw my life flash before my eyes during the accident. There are many things that it's imperative that I make changes to. I have a choice to change my present situation! I have been pondering

157

over many things since you have been here with me.
Mom, I forgive you for what happened concerning my
daughter. I accept your invitation to help me to look
for her and we will begin as soon as I am released
from here. Mom, thank you for allowing me to vent.
There are some things that I will have to place in
order. I pray that God will grant me a speedy
recovery. Has the doctor spoken with you concerning
my condition?" Sugar asked with anticipation.

"Well, Sugar I will not withhold any of the
information from you. Dr. Turner spoke with us,
before I entered in here. He stated you have paralysis
in your lower extremities; and he is uncertain whether
you will walk again. He stated that it will be a process.
He understands that you remain in the hands of the
Lord."

"Amen, Mom. God willing, I will walk again
and regain control over my life in all areas." Sobbing,

Sugar took in a deep breath to calm down. She wiped the tears from her eyes. "Right now I am feeling strong in my faith."

Gloria walked in, joining Doreen and Charlotte.

"I met Stanley in the hallway, heading back to the waiting area. He didn't look happy. What happened to the heart-warming fellow?" Gloria asked sarcastically.

"It appears that Stanley hasn't experienced being put in order often enough," Doreen expressed gladly.

"Yeah, Mom I truly understand that. I have been waiting for the opportunity to visit with my sister."

"I want to allow you all some time alone. Ok, Sugar," stated Doreen, "I will give you and your sister some time to visit together."

Doreen kissed Sugar on the cheek, said, "I love you," and proceeded to walk out the room.

"Sugar, girl, if you needed some attention, all you had to do was give me a call; you know I would have come over, brought you some coffee or just hung out with you. It wasn't necessary for you to come to the hospital for attention."

"Hahaha, funny!" stated Sugar. "You know if I had my choice I would not be here. There are a million things that I desire to be doing now, and there are a million places that I would rather be," Sugar stated in defense. "Where are my children, Gloria?"

"They are at my house with Jael."

"That's great, they always enjoy being in each other's company," Sugar stated calmly. "Gloria, I am really overjoyed that you are my second visitor for the evening. Stanley had the audacity to enter my room of peace and tranquility and demand that Mom leave so that he could have time to visit with me! I understand things and am seeing very clearly now. Life is short and can end in the twinkling of an eye. I deserve and desire happiness. I don't have the energy or the desire to deal with Stanley right now. I would just like to surround myself with people that bring pleasure instead of grief. Speaking of pleasure, have you heard from Fernando? I was speaking with him on the phone before my accident," Sugar stated.

Gloria nodded. "Fernando is in the waiting area."

"Gloria, I would like to see Fernando. I do not wish to see Stanley," Sugar appealed.

"Sugar, I will uphold your request at this time, especially since you have undergone so much with this current situation. When the doctor spoke with us, he stated we should not visit with you for an extended amount of time. He stated that you required your rest. I will bring Fernando back to see you and I will take care of Stanley for you. I will heed your request and inform the others that you need your rest."

Gloria walked down the corridor and headed to the waiting area.

"Gloria," stated Stanley, "I see that you finally decided to come out and allow others the ability to glimpse Sugar during this time."

"Well," Gloria began, "I am glad that I met you before returning to the waiting area; Sugar is tired, being so heavily sedated and she wishes to rest now. The doctor asked that we not stay for an extended period of time, but allow her to rest."

"Yes, I did hear the doctor say that. Ok. I will leave her to rest and return in the morning. I need to take Sister Candy home anyway. Will you let the other family members know as well?" Stanley inquired.

"Indeed I will," remarked Gloria.

That was easier than I thought. He left just like that, without putting up a fight. Perhaps what Mom said to him really permeated his heart.

"May I have the attention of the family and friends of Charlotte Spickley? Speaking on behalf of my sister, Charlotte, she will not be entertaining any more company this evening. She must get her rest. Thank you for coming and if you have brought any gifts, I will see that they are delivered to her room." Gloria spoke this loudly to capture the attention of everyone affected.

Gloria assured that all of the guests left for the evening. She then turned to Fernando, stating aloud,

"Will you take these cards and this plant quietly into Sugar's room, down this corridor to the right, Room 222?"

"Sure," exclaimed Fernando.

I can hardly wait to glimpse the love of my life, even if it is for but a moment. Fernando entered the room and appeared surprised that Sugar laid there with her eyes open. Fernando was so excited he could hardly contain himself. Fernando leaped from the doorway to her bedside and hugged her tightly.

"Hi Babe," Fernando squealed.

Sugar felt a warm rushing sensation that filled her whole being. Sugar glowed both externally and internally.

"Hello my love," replied Sugar.

"Sugar, I have longed for this moment ever since our conversation ended and I wasn't able to communicate with you. I don't know what I would have done if you were no longer in this earthly realm. I have been here ever since the ambulance brought you in. I have been interceding in prayer on your behalf. Darling, I am so moved and overjoyed that we are having this time together. I don't know if you have been told the prognosis of your injuries, but I truly believe and feel that you will rebound from this, my love. Once you rebound, you will be stronger as well. For there is nothing that is too hard for God! He blesses us to persevere through any storm! He would not have brought you to this place in your personal journey if He didn't believe that you had the ability to rise above it!"

"Yes, Fernando I am aware of the medical prognosis, and I concur with you. I am thankful that the baby is still growing inside of me," Sugar stated, staring directly into his eyes. "Fernando, one thing I know for certain is that since I have been confined to this bed and God has blessed me to come out of surgery, there are some things in my life that must change. I intend to live a peaceful life without added stress. Our homes should always be a habitat of tranquility. I lack this complete tranquility in the presence of Stanley. I have endured so many heartaches and disappointments with him. I know that we all have our flaws and I am by no means perfect. What has been assured is I have been granted a second chance at life and intend to live it to the fullest extent possible. Darling, I am beginning to feel very tired right now, I think it is the medication; please let's continue the discussion in the morning."

"Sure thing Sugar, my dear Charlotte. I am so pleased that all is well and God has smiled upon us.

See you in the morning," stated Fernando with great compassion.

Fernando skipped down the hall with extreme cheerfulness! "Thank you, Lord for all that you have done!" Fernando prayed. Fernando reached Gloria and stated, "It is well. We can depart and return in the morning."

"Fernando, that seems to be a great plan; I need to check on the kids anyway. Jessica and Akeem will be spending the night with me."

"Gloria, please call me in the morning to alert me of the time you will be arriving to the hospital. I also appreciate the opportunity that you presented for Sugar and me to have some time alone. I am indebted to you," stated Fernando, giving her a hug and a peck on the cheek.

"Fernando, you are most welcome. I always say love is one of those things that you can't explain and can't explain away," Gloria said as they departed for the evening.

Fernando entered his house. *I can hardly wait to shower and jump into bed. It has been a lengthy night.*

"And where have you been, Fernando?" snarled Brenda.

"Brenda, let's not start with that. I phoned you earlier alerting you that there was a critical accident on Interstate 9 and I would be late getting home due to being at the hospital," explained Fernando.

"Yes, Fernando I remember the conversation clearly and that was several hours ago. Normally, when you have an emergency that you respond to, you provide more feedback than you did for this accident. What was the difference?" Brenda demanded.

"Brenda, this was someone I know and please, I don't want to discuss it anymore right now, I just would like to take my shower and relax!"

"And?????... That's supposed to pacify me or in some way move me?" Brenda stated exasperated.

"Brenda, all I am saying to you is that I don't have the energy to argue with you tonight! Can't you just give me space and not be so unreasonable all the time?" as he politely excused himself. "Goodnight!"

Fernando prayed, "Lord, how long must I endure this? Again, we continue on this rocky road. It seems that she makes every effort to disrespect me as her husband. I don't know what to do to correct it. Can things be salvaged or are they too far gone? God, I know that all things are possible through you, but change happens through willing hearts. I know my heart is open and willing, but is Brenda's? It seems that I have a great deal of conflicting thoughts and emotions. Please help to bring all things to light. In Jesus' name, Amen."

Stanley entered the hospital early the next morning hoping to spend some time with Sugar prior to his early morning board meeting scheduled for 10:00 a.m. at the church. Stanley deliberated over the announcement that Dr. Turner spoke concerning Sugar's pregnancy. Was it possible that Sugar was concealing this pregnancy from him? Stanley puzzled

Two Hearts Torn...

over whether Sugar was secretly planning on aborting their child. Stanley was determined to get to the bottom of this matter!

"Good morning, Mr. Spickley," Nurse Nickols greeted warmly.

"Good morning," Stanley grunted. "Is Charlotte awake?"

"Yes, I just completed her morning vitals. By the way Dr. Valentine is working with her this morning and she will be here soon to make her rounds."

"Okay, thanks for that information."

Stanley's level of anxiety intensified as he reached the entryway of the door leading to Sugar. He took a deep breath when he entered the room.

"Good morning, Charlotte. How are you doing today?" Stanley stated expectantly, standing at the edge of her bed. "I was trying to see you yesterday evening, but we received word when Gloria left your room that you were not allowed to entertain anyone else, as the doctor stated you needed your rest. I understood, so I took Sis. Candy and we left the hospital."

"Well," Sugar stated snidely, "I heard that you had some company with you while you were here to visit with me. So how is Sister Candy doing?"

"Oh, Sis. Candy is doing well, she's sorry that you were not up to seeing her on yesterday. Did you receive the card and flowers she brought you?" Stanley questioned, smiling.

"Yes, I received all of the gifts that our family and friends left for me. Why was it so important to you that I received Sister Candy's gift?" Sugar verbalized hastily.

"I was just wondering is all; she was very upset that she wasn't able to see you yesterday, and she hoped the get well gifts she purchased would bring sunshine to such a gloomy day, considering the accident and all."

"Oh, ok, it just seemed more like you were defending Candy."

"No, that wasn't my intention at all," Stanley stated humbly.

"Sugar, how are you feeling? I understand that the doctor is reporting you may never walk again. The devil is a liar! We can touch and agree in prayer right now for your healing. I believe that God will heal you completely back to your pre-accident condition."

"Yes, Stanley I believe that God will heal me as well. I am awaiting God's report versus the doctor's report."

"Shall we pray?" questioned Stanley.

"Sure," agreed Sugar.

Stanley prayed, "Father, in the precious name of Jesus, we bow humbly before you at this time. We first would ask that you would forgive us for any sins that we've committed. We now come to you on behalf of my wife. God, you know everything about her condition, and you know what it will take for her to be able to walk again. I humbly ask that you will grant our request and allow her to walk again. We ask in the name of Jesus that all of her organs would function as they should and mobility be given to every extremity, in Jesus' name. We count it done, Amen!"

"Amen!" stated Sugar. "Thanks Stanley, I appreciate the prayer. It has been such a long time since we have prayed together. Seems that our lives have been drifting further and further apart. I remember our initial meeting and courtship; as I reflect it gives my heart joy. Although, I didn't receive the word from God as you did, I accepted that you were my husband, and I loved you more than life itself during that time. I desired to be your 'favor, your good thing.'

"I remember you saying, 'Sugar, I am proud to call you my wife, my favor, my completeness.' When you uttered those words, it pierced the deepness of my soul and spirit. There was nothing that I would have withheld from you at that time. But, now that seems to be such a distant memory...words spoken by you that have failed to be fulfilled and evident in my life today. I feel like a fool, just trusting that you would always protect me and care for me, have the willingness to meet my needs as a wife, as your lover. Stanley, you have disappointed me many times. I have felt the deepest hurt from the words you have uttered. It feels like you didn't even care how your words penetrated my heart.

"Stanley, I have been thinking a great deal while I have been here in the hospital. One thing that is paramount is that life is too short and can change in the blink of an eye. I had no idea when I left the house yesterday morning that I would not be returning back home later the same evening. Yesterday my life shifted completely! I am lying here paralyzed and I don't know what the future holds. This could possibly be a difficult journey. But I will persevere! I was unprepared; it took me completely by surprise! Stanley, I discerned an attitude from the way you entered my room this morning. I will not continue moving forward like I have been. I decree

and declare, it will not be business as usual in the

Spickley home. My voice and feelings will count!"

"Sugar, dear, it is true I did have an issue that I

wished to discuss with you during this visit. When Dr.

Turner gave us your prognosis on yesterday evening

he stated that the baby was doing fine. And, by his

estimation that you were about eight weeks pregnant.

I am happy to know the baby is fine, but why didn't

you tell me that you were expecting? Are we keeping

secrets from each other, now?"

"Stanley, perhaps that is a question you could

better answer. You have been very distant with me

these days. Furthermore, our children are almost

grown, and I am about to begin all over again with a

newborn. I am at the stage of life where I was

welcoming experiencing an empty nest in a few years.

Do you realize that Akeem and Jessica are almost

grown? They will be leaving our home soon and venturing off to experience life on their own. It isn't like you have been making me feel warm and fuzzy inside. Due to the distance felt in our marriage, there hasn't been a moment that I felt the freedom to share this new found information. So now that you have found out this information, what are your thoughts?"

"Well, Sugar initially I was thinking that I needed to put you in your place for withholding such important information from me," Stanley stated candidly.

"That's the problem, Stanley you always feel as though you sit in the high seat and are able to put people in their respective places! Sometimes it's better to have all the details before jumping to conclusions! It's better to know the whole matter."

Stanley opened his mouth to respond to Sugar's statements... Dr. Valentine entered the room.

"Good morning, Mr. and Mrs. Spickley. How are the two of you doing?"

"Well," they both answered in unison.

"Well, Mrs. Spickley, you had quite an ordeal on yesterday. I have all of your reports and we have discovered that you have some swelling in your central nervous system and that is what is causing the paralysis of your lower extremities. There is a new medication that we would like to begin using that will eliminate the inflammation in the central nervous system. This medication is administered weekly, and we are uncertain how long the process will be or if it will be effective. The drug will be administered directly into your spinal cavity and you must lie completely still during the administration of this medication. If you are in agreement with trying this experimental procedure, we can begin in the morning."

Dr. Valentine continued discussing measures available to eradicate Charlotte's prognosis...

Sugar thought, *I am thankful for my past nursing training, as I am able to follow the medical terminology associated with my illness. I can remember so vividly how we students were tasked with learning how deoxygenated blood travels into the heart from the body and travels through the heart walls into the lungs. Once blood is in the lungs it gathers oxygen, returns to the heart, and is distributed throughout the body. I reflect on chanting to myself, "Try to be right" (the tricuspid valve) is located on the right side of the heart. It's amazing how things learned in the past have a way of being useful during the present stage of life!*

"Mrs. Spickley, are you willing for us to begin the administration tomorrow?" Sugar nodded in agreement.

"Well, I will be covering for Dr. Turner for the remainder of tonight so if you need me, don't hesitate to have the nurses page me. Do you have any further questions?"

"No, Dr. Valentine," Charlotte and Stanley answered in unison.

Stanley rose from his chair. "Alright, Sugar I must leave you now. I need to head to the board meeting as we have a great deal of old business to discuss and resolve. I will be in touch later this evening to check on your progress. We will have time soon to discuss the pressing issues of our relationship!"

"Alright, Stanley I will speak with you soon."

181

Oh my gracious! My mind was going in so many directions with Stanley in here. He has a way of placing me on edge. I didn't even ask Dr. Valentine if that medication would have any negative effects on my fetus.

Hearing the phone ring, Sugar cleared her throat. "Hello," Sugar mustered, just above a whisper.

"Hello Sugar, how are you doing, precious? Did I catch you at a bad time? Are you in pain?"

"No, Gloria. Your brother-in-law and the doctor just left the room. And I didn't even ask the doctor if the recommendation of the treatment regimen would cause harm to my baby! I don't know how I did that. Already it looks as if I am an unfit mother."

"Sugar, Sugar please calm down, everyone knows that you are a very conscientious individual, and always concerned about the welfare of others. There is no way that you would not consider your unborn child. Now, what is the treatment regimen?"

"Oh, Gloria, please I don't wish to give you those gloomy details over the phone; besides you were calling me. How may I be of service?"

"Well, Sugar, just wanted to know if you were up for company? Fernando, has already called earlier this morning to see what time I would be coming over to visit you."

"Gloria, you know I always welcome your and Fernando's company. Especially after this morning, what a day! Please come over as soon as you are able," Sugar stated in agreement.

After Sugar finished her conversation with Gloria, she rang the call bell for assistance. It seemed a moment later Nurse Nickols was standing at her bedside.

"Yes, Mrs. Spickley, how may I be of assistance?" she stated accommodatingly.

"Earlier, Dr. Valentine came and discussed the next phase of treatment; however, being bombarded with this new information I failed to ask her a question. Is it possible that you could have her return later?"

"Sure, Mrs. Spickley."

"Thanks, Nurse Nickols."

"You are welcome; we aim to please. Are you comfortable? Is there anything else?"

"Yes, I am very comfortable. You really fixed me up the last time you were in here." Sugar smiled.

"No, you have been most helpful Nurse Nickols, please enjoy the rest of your day."

Whew. Now I can finally close my eyes and relax.

Chapter 10

Gloria and Fernando walked into Sugar's room. "Hello, beautiful lady!" Fernando greeted.

His voice is so sexy, it almost makes me melt, Sugar thought. *It is very moving.* At that moment she was feeling alive and felt her bodily juices being awakened. *It is refreshing to know that my paralysis doesn't affect my intimate feelings. I wonder if I would be able to carry through with these feelings in my new found condition.*

"Hello, Fernando. Thanks for the compliment; although, I feel like I was rolled over by a bus," Sugar mustered with a smile.

I know that I must look like who did it and why. I appreciate Fernando's ability to always make me feel like a million dollars. He always warms my heart.

"Hey girl, there is another person in the room! Remember, me Sugar, I am your younger, beautiful, angelic sister Gloria?"

"Hey Gloria, how could I ever forget you? I am happy to see the both of you."

"Really?" Gloria smiled. "You could have fooled me!"

"Fernando, there is some information that is paramount that I share with you. First, let me begin with the doctor's report. Dr. Valentine informed Stanley and me that there is an experimental medication they would like to begin implementing tomorrow. It was discovered that the swelling in my central nervous system is causing the paralysis of my lower extremities."

Gloria interrupted, "Where is this central nervous system? Remember, I lack the medical background."

"Oh, I'm sorry Gloria, the central nervous system includes the brain and the spine."

"Oh, wow, those are two of the most vital organs of the body."

"Yes, I know," Sugar continued. "So, I am not afraid of the drug; what is concerning me is the impact it will have on my unborn child. When Dr. Valentine was discussing the treatment regimen, I forgot to ask her about the pregnancy, Stanley had my head spinning in so many directions. I did ask the nurse to have her to return so I may address this issue."

"Yes, Sugar, I think it's best that we are assured that the baby will be okay," Fernando stated with much compassion and concern.

At that moment Dr. Valentine entered the room.

"Good afternoon, Mrs. Spickley; I understand you requested to see me?"

"Yes, I did, Dr. Valentine."

"Am I free to discuss your treatment regimen in the presence of your guests?"

"Yes, Dr. Valentine. This is my sister Gloria, and our dear family friend, Fernando."

"Very well," Dr. Valentine responded. "How may I be of service to you?"

"Will the medication have a negative effect on my fetus?" Charlotte asked in great anticipation.

"Mrs. Spickley, please rest your mind; I assure you when this treatment regimen was considered, we factored in the fact that you are expecting. We would not dare offer a treatment regimen without considering the health of your unborn child," assured Dr. Valentine.

"Dr. Valentine, you must understand, all of the trauma that I have been through I didn't assume all of my elements would be considered, I understand there is an element of uncertainty in all treatment regimens. I had to be sure that my unborn child would be safe," Charlotte voiced with great concern.

"Yes, Mrs. Spickley. I completely understand. I wasn't by any means trying to underestimate your feelings. Please understand that we will do everything possible scientifically to get you back to your optimal level of health and functioning," Dr. Valentine voiced empathetically.

"I appreciate you coming back to answer the questions that I had concerning my condition. Will you be here for the administration of the medication in the morning?"

"No, Dr. Turner will be here; he will return in the morning."

"Ok thanks, and do enjoy the rest of your evening, Dr. Valentine."

"Thank you, Mrs. Spickley, you enjoy yours as well, and I wish you great success during the surgical procedure in the morning."

"Thanks again for all your help, Dr. Valentine."

"My pleasure," Dr. Valentine verbalized, exiting the room."

"Well, Praise God!" Gloria screamed. "Lord, I thank you that the procedure will not have a negative impact on my niece or nephew."

"Amen," they all said in unison.

"Now, that we have heard the report, please continue with what you wanted to share with me," Fernando inquired.

"Well, this is a bit difficult, Fernando, this part of my life hasn't been disclosed to many people. I have yet to share it with Stanley. Isn't Stanley supposed to be the closest person in the world to me as my husband? Aren't we supposed to be one flesh?" Sugar took in a deep breath, and began to cry.

"Sugar, darling, whatever it is that you want to share with me, I will not judge; I will try to understand, and do all I can to assist you in making it better. Does this involve the pregnancy?"

Wiping her tears and hands shaking. "No Fernando, it doesn't involve my current pregnancy."

"Ok, I am listening, Sugar."

"Alright. About 30 years ago, I was dating a guy from school of whom I was very fond. During this time, I was a virgin, my family was very religious; as a matter-of-fact, my father was the associate minister at our church. My mother was actively involved in the church ministry as well. This young man and I began getting closer and a few months after we became sexually intimate, I became pregnant.

"My parents were outraged; I was presented two options: (1) to get married or (2) give the baby up for adoption. Well, I still remember the words uttered by my lover and love of my life, 'I am not prepared to be a daddy or a husband.' I was devastated! And to make matters worse, my parents sent me away to live with my aunt and uncle in Pennsylvania, so I would not cause shame to our family. I was required to give my daughter up for adoption. That was the hardest part of my life and now I want more than ever to have my daughter as an active part of my life. My children have no knowledge of having an older sister."

Before Sugar could utter another word, Fernando took her into his arms and just held her... Sugar wailed and wailed. Sugar thought, *I feel as light as a feather. What a release! For the first time when reflecting on this empty part of my life I felt complete protection. I now feel a deeper connection with Fernando. I feel that he understands the very essence of my being. Wow, what a connection!*

"Sugar, I can only imagine the weight this has caused you all of these years. I am here for you and we will figure out what the next step is together. I have a few connections in the Pennsylvania area.

194

Don't worry, babe, we will get through this and this too shall pass!"

"Thank you, Fernando."

"Now, Gloria and I are going to leave you so you may get the rest you need. You have had a long day and your body needs to prepare for the procedure in the morning. Gloria and I will return in the morning."

"Please guys, stay a little longer. I enjoy your company so much. By the way, Gloria, how are my kids?"

"Sugar, they are doing well."

"Good, I miss seeing my babies! Tell them mommy loves them."

Stanley hurriedly entered the board meeting, he knew they had been waiting for him for about an hour to bring the business meeting to order.

"Good morning board members, first of all I would like to apologize for my tardiness this morning. I have been at the hospital with my wife. For those of you who don't know, she was in a car accident a couple days ago."

"Oh my goodness," shouted Deacon Wilkins, "how is she doing?"

"Well, she has suffered quite a blow! She is paralyzed from the waist down. It may be a long road to complete recovery, God knows. Thanks for your concern. I trust that you have received a copy of today's agenda?"

"Yes, Pastor Spickley, I sent all of the board members the agenda and printed out a few," Sister Candy stated.

"Thanks, Sister Candy I can always depend on you to be efficient."

"Well, Pastor Spickley, I aim to please."

"Alright, let's begin with the old business, followed by new business."

Items on the agenda seemed to be resolved very quickly. All the board members were sitting in their respective places: Pastor Spickley at the head of the table with Sister Candy Willoughby to his right, as the recording secretary.

"Sister Willoughby, will you be so kind as to read the minutes of our last meeting?"

Sister Candy stood dressed in a fashion that commanded attention: a skin tight pin striped suit that accentuated her voluptuous curves.

"Good morning, excuse me, good afternoon board members, I rose to make the following report," Candy stated, ensuring her diction was precise. Candy ensured all the details were presented before the seven board members. After approximately 15 minutes Candy concluded the report. Candy glared into Pastor Spickley's eyes and awaited the motion that would excuse her.

Pastor Spickley quickly jumped to attention as Candy concluded the report of the minutes, "We have heard the reading of the minutes; is there a motion on the floor?"

Deacon Blake stood promptly. "I would like to make a motion to receive the minutes as read by Sister Candy with any necessary corrections."

"I second that motion," stated Dr. Claude. "I would like to add, Sister Candy, you are doing an exceptional job."

"Thank you, Dr. Claude," Candy stated, blushing.

"Well, Sister Candy, you are dismissed. You may take your seat."

"With pleasure, Pastor Spickley." She ran the backside of her hand beneath her, cupping the bottom of her skirt as she took her seat.

"Ummm hmmmm," Pastor Spickley cleared his throat. "Now that our board meeting has concluded, I would like to make the following announcement: We will have to postpone the fundraising campaign until next month as I am uncertain of the plight of my beloved Sugar concerning her health. She has to undergo an intrusive medical procedure in the morning. This fundraising campaign requires much time and attention and I don't have it to apply at this moment. Please understand this request."

The board members all stated in unison, "We are suspending the fundraising campaign at this moment." Deacon Wilkins stated, "If you require anything further, please don't hesitate to call us."

"Thanks, Deacon Wilkins, and will you please dismiss us in prayer?" requested Pastor Spickley.

"Sure, Pastor, I don't mind if I do." Immediately after the prayer ended, Sister Candy stated, "I noted the meeting adjourned at 1:02 p.m."

"Thanks, Sister Candy," stated Pastor Spickley. "I appreciate your efficiency."

Yielding a kind smile, Candy stated, "Pastor Spickley, may I please see you in your office? I have a personal issue that I need to discuss with you."

"Sure, Sister Candy."

Candy proceeded to walk in front of Pastor Spickley to be sure that he was able to get a court side view of what she had to offer. Candy made sure to walk in a fashion that would cause her backside to move up and down like two plump ripe cantaloupes. Candy meant business and she was prepared to handle the business matters discreetly.

"Ok, what is the matter you would like to discuss with me?"

"Well, Stanley I was wondering when will we be able to get together especially since you have suspended the fundraising campaign?"

Candy's eyes were speaking a love language of their own. Those eyes were beckoning for Stanley to come closer to have a taste and completely experience the sweetness of Candy.

Stanley expeditiously addressed Candy's forwardness. "It is difficult for me to fathom the notion of your insensitivity considering my wife's present condition! You are not being reasonable."

"Stanley, there are some things that you must understand. A woman like me requires a great deal of attention and if you are unable to fulfill my demands, I will have to move on. There is a raging fire burning throughout my body that needs to be quenched! I am tired of using that box of toys to bring myself to ecstasy! I am craving you! Isn't it possible for us to have another secret board meeting of our own?"

"Not at this time, and if you are unable to wait until I will be able to move forward, please carry on."

"Stanley, you sure make it seem that you have nothing to be afraid of if I walk away from you. Are you considering the ministry and what the people will say if this information happened to leak out?"

"Candy, I am not concerned about that as you will have just as much to lose, being that your husband is battling prostate cancer. How will you explain creeping out on him in his condition? Is he still requiring three days of chemotherapy to treat his condition?"

"Well, actually he is receiving radiation treatment once a week. So, Stanley are you saying you are calling my bluff?"

"No, I am not calling your bluff! I am saying that you need to calm down and let me have some time. Sugar has to have a medical procedure tomorrow that has the potential of being detrimental. I don't need any more pressure at this time."

"Ok, Stanley, I will give you some time, but just know that I am ready to ride that horse again."

"I understand, Candy; I am just asking for some understanding from you at this time."

"Well, Stanley you know when Calvin and I met, we both had a past. Both of our lives haven't been squeaky clean. He knows that I require intimacy and have massive needs! But I will entertain your request for now."

Sugar took in a deep breath as she prayed, "Father God, I believe that you possess the ability to heal me completely through this medical procedure, I fully place my life in your hands. Oh, you are the air I breathe! You are the lover of my soul, Jesus! I believe that all is well, in Jesus' name."

"Mrs. Spickley, what are you doing awake, at 4 o'clock in the morning?" Nurse Nickols asked while entering her room.

"Yes I am aware of the time. I am unable to sleep; I have been awake for an hour now. I am anticipating the operation. This is my first hospital stay due to illness or injury. I have only been hospitalized during the delivery of my children. I have been praying, but only God knows what the full manifestation will be following the surgery," Sugar stated.

"Mrs. Spickley, Dr. Turner is a very experienced surgeon who has been practicing for over 30 years; he is more than capable of performing the surgery," Nurse Nickols stated in an effort to console her.

"Nurse Nickols, I appreciate you saying that; however, there is no way a mortal man can replace the hand of God. I understand that you were attempting to console me, place my mind at ease, and I know that it came from a good place," Sugar stated compassionately. "I acknowledge all of your acts of kindness."

"Thanks, Mrs. Spickley, now try to get your rest. You will be having surgery in approximately 5 ½ hours. You will be taken down for preparation of the procedure about a half hour before the surgery begins," Nurse Nickols stated with much warmth.

"Sugar... good morning, Sugar."

"Huh, huh," Sugar managed to muster, rolling over, groggy.

"Hello, sissy," stated Gloria. "We wanted to come and see you before the surgery."

"Who is the 'we' Gloria?" Sugar stated with a raspy voice, "I only see one of you standing here."

"I have the children out in the waiting room, I wanted to be sure that you were in condition to see them before bringing them in."

"Yes, Gloria," Sugar squealed, "please bring in my babies."

"Ok, Sugar I will do so as you requested; however, I would like to inform you that both Fernando and Stanley are in the waiting room."

"Alright, thanks for the warning. Gloria, you are awesome. I thank you for never judging me and always having a desire to see clearly into my experiences. I appreciate you being family and a confidant."

"Sugar, you don't have to say that! You know I have your back and I love you unconditionally beyond measure. I treasure our relationship and the love we share; you too have always been in my corner."

"Alright, enough with the mushy talk; bring my babies in."

It seemed at a moment's notice that Gloria was back in her presence with Akeem and Jessica.

"Hi, Momma. How are you doing?" shouted Akeem.

"Yeah," Jessica chimed in, "we miss you and we love you. We have been praying for God to heal you."

"Thanks, baby. Momma loves the both of you, too. I am glad your Aunt Gloria brought y'all to see me before my surgery."

"Okay, kids let's allow some of the other family members to come in and visit with your mother before she's taken off to surgery."

Gloria walked down the hall to the waiting area and she witnessed a flood of people gathered to see Sugar before the surgery. Gloria smiled inside and out. People were in and out of Sugar's room taking their time to show her love.

Sugar felt so much love at this moment. "God, I thank you for the favor you have bestowed upon me! I am grateful for all the love shown to me during this time."

Sugar thought, *Of course it was such a pleasure to see Fernando again. I imagine how it*

would feel to hold him again and have him hold me
again. With so many people around, and Stanley
being present, it was impossible to act on any of
these feelings. I know that it is important to keep my
feelings at bay. I felt a bit of relief being surrounded
by family and friends. My anxiety level seemed to
almost melt completely away.

Nurse Tammy entered the room, "Mrs. Spickley, it's time for your surgery. Are you ready?"

"Well," Sugar replied, taking in a deep sigh, "as ready as I will ever be. Let's get this over with."

Nurse Tammy rolled her down the hallway; she passed her family and friends they responded by saying their good-byes in unison wishing her a speedy recovery and a productive surgery. Sugar was smiling.

Stanley ran up to her bedside, "Sugar, darling, I will be here when you return from your surgery."

Really? Was it necessary for Stanley to put on such a stellar performance? Whose convenience was this announcement made for? I am not about to allow him to spoil this moment. He can put on the performance of his choosing! Next!

"Alright Stanley," Sugar stated warmly.

Chapter 11

Hearing the phone ring... *Oh my goodness, this phone has been ringing nonstop. Wonder who it is now?* "Thank you for calling *Beautiful Diva's*, Sally speaking, how may I direct your call?"

"How are you doing, Sally? This is Brenda. I was calling to check on things at the shop. Have you been able to link all of my clients with the other stylists? As it stands now it looks like I will be out for six weeks. I do intend on coming in periodically to check on things, but just wanted to reach out and touch base today."

"I am doing well, and I am so happy to hear from you. Regarding your first question, yes, I have been able to link all of your clients and reschedule your appointments as you instructed. Also, the contracting agency called stating they are very sorry for the damages they caused, and they would like to settle with you out of court. I have that information for you as well in your work mailbox. The contractors further delivered the legal information through certified mail with a signature request."

"Well, if those bozos think that I'm about to settle out of court, they have another think coming, with all of this pain and suffering that I'm enduring at this moment. No way! Sally, why did I have to call in to the salon today? Did I not instruct you to contact me daily to give me a rundown of what's going on in the office?"

Sally took in a deep breath; she didn't want to verbalize to Brenda the way that she was feeling at this moment. *She is such a micromanager!* "Brenda, I wanted you to get your rest; after all, you are recuperating after a tragic accident. We thank God that it's as well as it is because it certainly could have been much worse."

"Sally, thank you for your concern, but I didn't need all of that extra. When were you planning to alert me regarding the legal certified mail?"

"Brenda, you know that I share all of the business's information with you. As I stated previously, I wanted you to rest."

"Ok, so what items are on the agenda today?"

"Well, all of the stylists are in today and continue working at being productive. The new massage therapist presented; however, I sent her home due to the incomplete renovations on the spa area. There wasn't ample space for her to work or to have the privacy needed for our clientele."

"Yes, I understand that. Duh, that is why the renovations have been initiated. Did *Exquisite Renovations* call to give a quote?"

"Yes, they called earlier and left a message, but it has been so busy that I haven't been able to return their call."

"Sally, I was afraid something like this would happen if I wasn't there to oversee the business. I have renovations that are needed urgently. It continues to cost me more money. What do you suppose I should do about losing so much money, Sally?"

Sally pondered, *Does Brenda really think that she is the only capable person?* Sally had been working since 6:00 a.m. that morning trying to put everything in place before the salon doors opened at

7:00 a.m. Her sacrifices continued to go unnoticed
and unappreciated.

"Well, Brenda, I will be sure to contact them so
we can move on with the renovations as you desire."

"Ok, Sally, thank you for your efforts. I have to
understand that there is only one Brenda Storm;
therefore, my thinking will not be your thoughts."

"I appreciate you saying that, Brenda. Also, the
massage therapist stated she would contact you as she
lost commissions today; she had ten massages
scheduled."

"I know she's not trying to call me regarding
losses; I have lost the ten customer sales today as well.
I will deal with her when she calls. Sally, before we
conclude this call, has the management meeting been
rescheduled for next Wednesday?"

"Yes, Brenda, I have already informed all of the workers of that. I have already given them an agenda for the meeting as well."

"Great. Thanks for that. If I am unable to come in person we will conduct the meeting through skype or video conferencing instead. I like to view the facial expressions of people while conducting meetings."

"Alright, Sally that is all for now. I will talk with you soon. I must rest now, the medication is kicking in and I am getting drowsy."

"Alright, Brenda, take care and feel better. Looking forward to speaking with you soon. Bye for now."

"Ok bye." *Finally, that has ended! I thought she would never stop.*

Dr. Turner called into the family waiting room for surgical patients.

"Hello, you have reached the Spickley family."

"Hello, this is Dr. Turner; may I speak with Stanley Spickley, please?"

"Sure," the pleasant voice on the other end of the phone responded. "Stanley, it's Dr. Turner."

Stanley hurried over to the telephone receiver with much anticipation, "Hello, yes, this is Stanley. Is everything alright?"

"Hello, Mr. Spickley, this is Dr. Turner, the surgery seems to be very successful. It took us about an hour and a half. She tolerated the medication very well. Now, Mrs. Spickley is in the recovery room; she has been sedated, but she should be open to receive the family in about 30 minutes. Now we will see once she recovers where we stand for the conclusion of the first treatment. We will be able to determine whether the surgery was productive or not. Or, better yet, how many administrations we will need to provide for her."

"Okay. Thank you, Dr. Turner."

"You are most welcome, Mr. Spickley, I will be available through the hospital's on-call system. I will send the nurse out to get you all when she recovers."

"Thank you. I appreciate all you have done."

It seemed to Stanley like more than 30 minutes passed before Nurse Linda came out to greet the family and escort the first two family members to Sugar's room.

"Greetings, Spickley family. May I have the first two family members who would like to visit with Mrs. Spickley?"

All of the family members turned to Stanley; they wanted to figure out his process of thinking, especially since it appeared he always wanted to be in control of everything. "Who would like to accompany me as I visit with Sugar?" he asked with a smile as big as a Cheshire cat's.

After about two minutes of silence, Doreen stood, "I will gladly accompany you for the visit."

Nurse Linda walked ahead of them. "Right this way!"

They entered the room. Sugar was lying on her side facing the window.

"Good afternoon, Sugar," they said in unison.

"Hello, Stanley and hello, Mom. I am happy to see both of you."

"Yes, darling," Doreen exclaimed, "I thank God that He brought you safely through the surgery!"

"Yes, Mom; my sentiments exactly!"

Sugar thought, *I am happy and full of comfort to have my mom by my side again. It seems funny that just days ago I was full of so much animosity, hurt, and pain; now today I can embrace her with love overflowing in my heart. I feel like I can finally let my hair down and be at peace. It is amazing having my mom in my presence again. It feels like nothing can interrupt the warm, heartfelt sensation of this moment, and it is interesting to witness how far my mom and I have traveled in this journey called life.*

Stanley interrupted the moment of thought. "I am so thankful that you are feeling better and you are with me. I know that I haven't been the best husband, but I would like for us to work through our marital issues. If we have to go to a marriage counselor, I am willing to do so. One thing this accident has shown me is life is too short!" Stanley verbalized with great compassion.

"Yes Stanley, you are right, life is indeed short. And I am determined to live it to the fullest here in this earthly realm. Stanley, I know that we are married and as a couple we're supposed to be as one. I feel that we have grown so far apart, and I'm not sure if we are at the point of salvaging our marriage. I know that our marriage needs a lot of healing. Stanley, I have been suffering greatly as you have hurt me extremely bad, and it has been distressing to the point of my heart aching and bleeding for years. I feel that I have been starving for your love. Yearning for you to love me the way I have shown love.

"Stanley, I guess the most important question to ask is, are you feeling this way now because I'm lying in this bed paralyzed? You have uncertainty as to whether I will walk again? Perhaps my life will be cut short? You now want to step up to the plate to show your sheep the compassion you are extending to your darling wife? Perhaps the medication administered during the surgery will not fully reduce the swelling? Or are you reaching out because you truly want to have me be in your life completely, being your rib? Let's take it slow, Stanley, for as you see I just have so many questions. Just many unresolved feelings and issues. Let's just enjoy this day."

Sugar extended her hand to Doreen, put her hand inside Doreen's hand, looked her straight in the face. "Mom, I'm so glad that you are here!"

It was as if time stood still. Sugar took in deep breaths as she reflected on the moment. *I feel like I am surrounded by so much love. I feel as if the hand of God is upon my life and He is outpouring so much favor in it.*

Doreen broke the silence, "Alright, baby, we must leave you now. We have been here long enough and there are others who want to visit with you."

"Oh!" Sugar hollered out.

"What's wrong?" Doreen and Stanley questioned in unison.

"I am feeling a tingling sensation radiating down my legs. Please help me! Call the nurse!"

"Sure." Doreen rang the call bell to alert the nurse. It seemed in a moment's notice, Nurse Linda was standing in the room.

"Yes Mrs. Spickley, how may I be of assistance to you?"

"Nurse Linda, I have just begun feeling a tingling sensation radiating in my lower extremities."

"Mrs. Spickley, that is wonderful, it means that you have begun experiencing positive results from the surgery."

"Thanks, Nurse Linda; I feel so relieved. I didn't know if it was a complication as a result of the surgery."

"No, Mrs. Spickley it means that we are moving in the right direction. It confirms that the surgery was a success. I will alert Dr. Turner of the great news!"

"Wow," Sugar stated. "I appreciate your help."

"Certainly, Mrs. Spickley, is there anything else that I may do for you at this moment?"

"No, that is all for the moment. Oh my goodness, Mom and Stanley, I am feeling so overjoyed. My surgery was a success! Thank you, Jesus!"

"Sugar, I too am elated," Doreen verbalized with a wide smile.

"We are on our way to recovery," Stanley chimed in.

The next set of visitors to grace Sugar with their presence were Gloria and Fernando.

Whew! Sugar sighed as Fernando and Gloria entered the room. *Isn't that a breath of fresh air, my tall glass of drinking water!*

Sugar was so excited she was bouncing on the bed, "Hey, you guys, I have great news to share with you."

"What is that Sugar?"

"Well I was feeling a tingling sensation radiating down my legs, so I called the nurse because I thought perhaps something had gone wrong with the surgery. When she entered and performed an assessment to ascertain what the problem was, it was determined that the surgery was a success. I am having some feeling in my legs now."

"Well, Sugar, that is great news!" they both said, almost screaming with excitement.

"Now I need you both to take a seat; I have a lot to get off my chest. As you are aware Stanley and Mom visited first. Stanley proposed that we needed to begin marital therapy in an effort to fix our marital problems. I have many questions and reservations about his request, and I shared many of the questions with him.

"My dear Sugar, please let me speak," stated Fernando. "I know that you are hurt, but perhaps you need to consider the therapy so that you all can iron out your differences. So you are able to move on with clarity of thought. To figure out if you want to remain with Stanley and to investigate whether your marriage will work."

"So what about our relationship, Fernando?"

"Sugar, no doubt I love you, but we took vows with our spouses and I don't want to stand in your way of making a determination of whether your relationship is destined to last."

"Now, I am more confused, but I will think about it."

Gloria chimed in, "Sugar, I think whatever you decide it should be your decision; after all, you ultimately must be satisfied with the decision."

"Yes, Gloria, I think you are right."

Sugar continued entertaining company following her first surgical procedure. She remained in an elated, elevated mood for the remainder of the day. As a matter-of-fact, it appeared as though she didn't require much pain medication as a result. According to medical science it is likely the dopamine in the brain exhibited a high volume of happiness and it contributed to Sugar requiring less medication.

Sugar was overjoyed that so many of her family and friends turned out for her surgical procedure.

Just like anything else as time moved on, Sugar's condition seemed very hopeful, and although additional surgical procedures were scheduled, less and less of the family members were present. The only consistent family and friends who visited were Stanley, Gloria, Doreen and Fernando. This was understood and expected as people dwindled when they perceived things were going well. Sugar's car accident proved a sense of urgency, an emergency and more people were present, due to the uncertainty as to whether her life would be lost or sustained.

I thank God for all of my social support, Sugar thought. *As I reflect on many of the individuals in the community I serve, with mental illness there is not a great deal of social support. Many of the relationships are abusive and self-serving. It appears that my clients struggle with the ability to maintain healthy relationships and have adequate boundaries. Failing to maintain boundaries continues to plague individuals and cause them to spiral in a downward motion.*

It didn't seem that a month has passed since my hospitalization, five surgical procedures, combined with physical therapy, as it was imperative that my muscles continue to be utilized. In my opinion East Side Regional Medical Center hospital possesses a great physical therapy department, as well as nursing staff, I had a schedule so intense I thought I was working daily. That kept me active and that is what I needed. Just like anything else if you don't use it, you lose it. To be at this stage is completely a miracle. A month ago, I didn't know when the day would come when I would be walking independently and anticipating

discharge.

"Good afternoon, Mrs. Spickley," Nurse Nickols, stated while entering the room. "I have come with your discharge paperwork and the instructions concerning medication, follow-up with your primary care physician, recovery time, and activities that you may slowly resume. Mrs. Spickley, be sure that you do not engage in sexual intercourse for the next two weeks."

"What? Nurse Nickols, you do realize that I have been looking in you all's faces for the past month? You realize it has been awhile and I still must endure more agony? Do you realize how much of a release I need?"

"Mrs. Spickley, I am sorry. I don't mean to cause you more distress; please don't shoot the messenger."

"No, Nurse Nickols, I understand you are doing your job, I just needed to vent. Please continue with my discharge instructions. By the way, has my husband arrived?"

"No, Mrs. Spickley, he phoned earlier stating there was a situation beyond his control and he stated your sister, Mrs. Pettaway, will be coming for you this morning."

Well, isn't this wonderful, and convenient, Stanley? He didn't even have the decency of contacting me directly to alert me of the change. Really, Stanley? Requesting that the nurse notify me of this change during my discharge paperwork. Also, contacting my sister while he was doing all of his calling; wouldn't it have been simpler to contact me? Well, anyway, I am over him!

"Alright, Mrs. Spickley," Nurse Nickols interrupted Sugar's pattern of thought, "that concludes all of your discharge instructions. Do you have any questions for me?"

Is she serious? Please, spare me, the main question that I needed her to address she couldn't!

Sugar mustered a smile, "No, Nurse Nickols, I don't have any questions, as you have been most helpful. You all have been an excellent staff, if you please, a home away from home. Well, if that is possible. I am so ready to leave you! So, please send in my sister and we will not tarry; we will move expeditiously."

"Most certainly, Mrs. Spickley, I will miss you!"

"Thank you, Nurse Nickols. I will miss you too, but a good miss!" They both laughed.

In the blink of an eye, Gloria stood before Sugar and Nurse Nickols.

"Sugar, I have your getaway car; your personal wheelchair," Gloria stated, then laughed. "Good morning, Sugar; how are you this morning?"

"I am doing excellent, sis, so ready to be leaving East Side Regional."

"I hear you, sis."

"Well, shall we?"

"Yes, we shall." Sugar stated. As they entered the car, Sugar questioned, "Gloria, so, how did Stanley ask you to pick me up at the hospital?"

"Well, Sugar, he called me early this morning stating that there was a family emergency with one of the members of the church, with a husband and wife. He stated there was no one available to assist in this matter and he had to attend to it. Of course, I told him that it would be no problem picking you up. I sent the kids off to school as usual this morning. And I sat down at my computer beginning my work, before entertaining his call."

"Okay Gloria, whatever! Before we go to the house please take me by Chick-fil-A. I can just taste that chicken deluxe combo with coleslaw, and a bottled water. The hospital food has been okay, but it's nothing like a Chick-fil-A sandwich."

Chapter 12

Fernando rushed into the home; he entered the foyer area, and almost tripped over a new table that had mysteriously appeared in the middle of the foyer.

"What is this? This table wasn't here this morning."

"Fernando, is that you?" Brenda yelled from the kitchen.

"Yes honey, it is me. When did this table get here?"

"Oh, I had it delivered this morning."

"Well, Brenda why was I not consulted in this decision?"

"Really, Fernando? I can't believe you have the audacity to ask me that? Since when do I consult you when making decisions?"

"Brenda, I would have thought after all these years have passed and as much as we have gone through in this marriage that you would be willing to compromise sometimes. But then again, who am I kidding? This is who you are; perhaps one day it will truly sink in, and I will understand the true Brenda Storm."

"Well Fernando, I think you just had an Aha moment! Let me allow you to reflect on your last statement. By the way, it's very nice of you to grace me with your presence during your lunch hour," she stated sarcastically. Is it some special occasion that I am unfamiliar with? It has been about a month since you have come home during your lunch hour. I know this, because I have been recuperating for the past four weeks."

"Brenda, seriously? What does it matter whether or not I come home during my lunch hour? After all, it is ultimately up to me to choose, correct?"

"Well Fernando, you are always the first to state that I'm being irrational and uncompassionate! What about this behavior? During this time I have been stationary here due to my ankle; hardly able to finagle my way around the house, and you didn't even have the decency to call or come home and check on me during your lunch hour."

"Brenda, you can't be serious! Since when has it been an issue concerning my whereabouts, especially during my lunch hour? Matter-of-fact it seems as though you just tolerate me or I'm just in the way. So what is the true purpose behind you preparing lunch today? Perhaps there is something that you want of me?"

"Well, Fernando, since you mentioned your willingness to help, there is something that I require some assistance with."

"Exactly! That is my point. What is it this time, Brenda?"

"Fernando, as you know I have not been able to report to the salon as I desire since I have been here healing, recuperating following the accident."

"Brenda, am I to believe that you haven't made any unexpected trips to the salon? I don't mean to sound offensive, but Brenda, you are the master micro manager."

"Yes, Fernando I have been unable to make trips as I have been heavily sedated on the medication. I have been conducting our staff meetings via video conference calls. During our last conference call there were a few discrepancies found, and you know that I have to follow everything that my staff does with a fine tooth comb. I am not about to allow my business to be held captive in incapable hands. Now, the issue is, I have another construction company scheduled to come in and provide an assessment of the work that needs to be completed. After all, I have already lost much money since my spa area wasn't completed when anticipated and those appointments had to be cancelled. I would be grateful if you would be available to meet them and ensure the company isn't trying to get over on me. The company is Exquisite Renovations Construction Company."

"When are they scheduled to be there, Brenda?" Fernando stated nonchalantly.

"They are scheduled to be there tomorrow at 9:00 a.m."

"Ok, Brenda, sure. I will make arrangements to take care of that."

"Thanks, Fernando, I can always depend on you!"

"Yes, that is correct. By the way I did see that there was a check that was issued from Perkins Construction Company; shall we discuss that?"

"Well, Fernando if you must know that was a check for the injuries, pain, and suffering I sustained during that critical accident they wished to settle with me out of court. Further, my lawyer suggested that I take the settlement because they were very gracious. After all, what girl couldn't use an extra $50,000? It's the least that the construction company could do with all of the chaos they have caused. Perkins Construction has also taken care of my medical and legal fees. Some people may say that I should have requested $75,000 or $100,000, but I understand the more it is the more it's taxed. So this settlement is more profitable and rewarding, considering the circumstances."

"Brenda, I'm happy that you are sharing this with me now, but if I had not discovered the check, would you have opened up to me? These are some of the questions that continue to plague me! There are so many uncertainties as to whether you truly love me."

"Fernando!" Brenda screamed. "Here we go again, I don't have time for these terms of endearment moments that you always want to create! I mean really, Fernando? Are you on your period or something? Perhaps you are having a midlife crisis. I am tired of going through this additional stress. I am trying to heal; my bones are still in the process of fusing back together. I have been here looking at the four walls in this house for the past four weeks! I haven't even been able to go in to the salon to work, supervise, or to fully be aware of what's happening there. That is why I wanted you to go for me to meet Exquisite Renovations, as well as to check up on the staff. Fernando! If I can't trust you or depend on you to be there when I need you, then what are you good for?"

"Yeah, Brenda, I must accept that you have shown me who you are. In the words of the great motivational speaker, teacher in her own right, and a phenomenal woman, Dr. Maya Angelou, 'When people show you who they are, believe them.'"

Sugar walked into her house, looked around as if it was her first time being there. Sugar was careful to take in every angle of the house. Sugar thought, *It feels almost like a strange environment, but everything looks intact the way I left it. Including a few dirty dishes in the sink. Really? Is that my welcome home gift? I have discussed many times with all of the members of the household, the true essence of maintaining an appropriate housing environment. Well, I am not going to focus on that right now.* Sugar took in a deep breath.

"Are you okay, Sugar? What's wrong?" Gloria questioned attentively.

"Yes, Gloria, I am doing wonderful. I was just looking around the house and noticed the dishes in the sink. But Gloria, I understand I have to take care of myself. One thing is for sure, I don't have any babies in this house. At least for the time being," pointing to her stomach with a smile, Sugar stated.

"Sugar, it brings me so much delight to see you finding such joy in being pregnant. After all, I will be gaining a niece or nephew!"

"Gloria, I am prepared to put on my big girl panties and live with the hand that I have been dealt! I realize and understand there are consequences to every behavior. I walked into this situation with my eyes open and I am prepared to deal with the consequences. I will soon call the doctor to set up a paternity test and move forward. Why cry over spilt milk? The deed has been done."

"Sugar, I truly admire your confidence and your position on the issue. I lack your strength in that area; I would be so concerned and consumed with the thoughts of others. Sugar, you know the church will have a major issue if they discover you have indiscretions."

"Gloria," Sugar stated softly, "I understand your reservations, but I have matured; I understand that God is my judge. Contrary to the beliefs of others, God is the only one with the capacity and capabilities to judge my behavior. He will not be unjust and He will judge with compassion, wisdom, knowledge, and discernment of the full matter. Gloria, I have graduated from people and have my certificate to prove it! I am so over people being self-righteous as if they have been positioned through God to assist Him in judging. I am so over people with their self-serving agendas!"

"Sugar, that is why you are my mentor and role-model. I have so much respect for you. I thank God for allowing you to be a part of my life."

"Gloria, I thank God for the place you have in my life as well. Will you be a dear and hand me the phone? I am not going to procrastinate, I am prepared to face the music and pay the piper. I intend on calling the doctor's office to set up the paternity test." Sugar reached for the phone that Gloria was handing her. Her cell phone began ringing.

"Hello," Sugar stated, a bit startled.

"Hello, Sugar are you alright?"

"Oh, yes Fernando, besides having a little pain I am fine."

"Darling, I would like to see you. Are you still at the hospital?"

"No, Fernando, I have not too long ago made it home, Gloria is here with me."

"Where is Stanley?"

"He had an emergency and wasn't available to transport me from the hospital."

"Sugar, would it be okay for me to come over? I really need to see you."

"Sure, come on over."

"Well, Sugar, it's going to take an hour before I can get there."

"Yeah, Fernando, I know. No problem; Gloria is here with me."

"Alright babe, I'll see you soon!" Fernando stated excitedly.

Fernando thought… *I am very ecstatic that my sweetie has recuperated to the point of coming home.*

Sugar thought... *It has been a long journey, but I am pleased with the results of the journey. It could have been far worse! I am up and walking around. God, I praise you for your healing power! I praise you for bringing me to this picture of optimal health!*

Sugar's thought was interrupted by Gloria. "What are you doing inviting him to come here to see you?"

"Gloria, I'm inviting him to come here because I would like to see him. I'm a big girl. Besides, you do realize the whole time I was at the hospital that when Fernando visited basically the two of you were together?"

"Yes Sugar, but of course everybody knows that my husband was overseas and recently came back from being deployed."

"Yeah I know, so it gives the appearance that he's visiting the both of us, and he is a friend of ours. In reality he's an intimate friend/lover of mine."

"Well, Sugar I am not about to get involved in the way you choose to handle your affairs. I continue being supportive of your endeavors. You know I am here for you."

"Correct, little sis. I thank you, and I truly appreciate you; you definitely bring value to my life. By the way, during the last meeting with my lover he extended an open flight ticket to Ocho Rios, Jamaica and after I am cleared physically from my medical restrictions, I wish to accept his request and travel. As you can imagine I have been under a great deal of stress after being hospitalized for a month, being pregnant, and continuously dealing with Stanley's foolishness! I would like you and Samuel to travel with us, and I would like us to travel next month, before I am too enormous! At this stage of pregnancy, it is difficult for anyone to detect and I will be more apt to enjoy the experience."

"So, Sugar, you wish to travel in the next few weeks?"

"Yes Gloria, that is correct for the reasons expressed. Do you anticipate that being a problem?"

"Well Sugar, let me discuss it with Samuel, it may be a possibility. Are you sure you want to travel with Samuel being as he will perceive the intimacy shared between you and Fernando?"

"One thing I know to be true about Samuel is that he thinks outside the box and isn't judgmental, as he tries to gather all of the information before quickly leaping to opinions and biases. I further feel that he has discerned that things are not peachy between Stanley and me. Gloria, I ask that you present the information to Samuel and allow him to make the determination. Gloria, things are going to be different around here! Stanley continues treating me the way that he has, because I have allowed him to. He is about to be exposed to a different Sugar."

Sugar finished her statement and the doorbell to the front door rang. *Wonder who that could be?* Sugar thought. "Do you mind getting the door for me, Gloria?"

"Sure, Sugar," she stated, rising from her seat. Gloria opened the door and was greeted by Fernando stating, "Isn't this a pleasant surprise?"

Fernando entered the house. Sugar became so excited, she could hardly contain herself, which was obvious by her smiling and sitting on the edge of the seat as if she were preparing to be ejected from a flight!

Gloria thought, *If I didn't know any better I would have thought that this was the first time Sugar had seen him since the accident.* Gloria reflected Fernando visited every day at the hospital for the past month. Perhaps it was just so comforting to have Fernando in her presence in a more intimate and relaxed setting.

Sugar finally managed to stand from the sitting position. Sugar thought... *Pre-accident the lowness of chairs had no effect on my ability to get up and down, post-accident I now realize it's a process of getting out of the chairs as I stand.* Sugar embraced Fernando fully and they kissed. Sugar thought, *Wow what a kiss! At this moment I am feeling everything within this mortal body becoming aroused and alive.*

"Fernando, it is so good seeing you again," Sugar stated in her sensual voice. *It feels so good to have another meeting with my lover!* "Fernando, please take a seat. Now that you are here we can begin placing things into perspective. So, first of all I would like to call Dr. Peters' office to schedule a paternity test. I want to know whose child I am carrying!"

"Sugar, whew, that is like a breath of fresh air! I very much want to know as well. That will be the deciding factor on how we need to proceed with our lives!"

"Yes, indeed it will," Sugar agreed.

"Well, there is no time like the present!"

"Wow, Sugar I like this new side of you. Sometimes, sorry to say this, you procrastinate!"

"Yes, Fernando, that is true, but no more; it's time to turn over a new leaf. I am ready to live life to the fullest!"

"Good afternoon, thank you for calling Dr. Peters' office, Lula speaking, how may I direct your call?"

"Yes, good afternoon, Lula; may I please speak with Dr. Peters?"

"Hold the line, please. Yes, may I ask who is calling?"

"Sure, it is Mrs. Spickley."

"Ok, let me see if he is available. Mrs. Spickley?"

"Yes, I am here."

"Transferring to Dr. Peters."

"Good afternoon, Mrs. Spickley. How may I assist you?"

"Dr. Peters, it is a pleasure speaking with you."

"Yes, I understand you were discharged this morning."

"Yes, I was happy that you were able to continue my prenatal care while I was hospitalized."

"Yes, Mrs. Spickley that is all a part of my duties and responsibilities. I aim to reach the needs of the massive number of patients and I have been known to make house calls."

"Wow, really? I will definitely keep that in mind for the future. Ok, Dr. Peters I would like to make an appointment for the paternity testing."

"Alright, well we perform those tests on Wednesdays and Fridays. Which day will be better for the two of you?"

There was a brief pause. Sugar glanced over to Fernando, "Which day is better for you?"

"Friday is good for me."

"Okay, Dr. Peters, Friday will be the best day."

"Alright, can you be here at 11:00 a.m.?"

"Sure, that will be fine."

"Alright, Mrs. Spickley. I will see you then."

"Thanks, Dr. Peters, and have a great day."

"Thanks and the same to you, Mrs. Spickley."

"Well, now that matter is taken care of, let's move to the next thing. Gloria and I were discussing the possibility of the four of us: Gloria, Samuel, you and me, traveling to Jamaica next month."

"Ok, the latter part of the month will be better for me, July 19th-August 2nd," stated Fernando, looking down at his pocket calendar.

"That works for me," Sugar stated. "Gloria, when you present the idea to Samuel, will you please consider those dates?"

"Sure, Sugar that will not be a problem."

Sugar thought... *Each time Fernando is in my presence, it seems as if time stands still. I feel totally and completely comfortable when he is around.*

Fernando sat quietly stroking Sugar's hair and holding her in his arms. Fernando interrupted the silence. "Well, my dear Sugar, as much as I am enjoying the moment it is 7:00 p.m. and I must get home."

"Alright, Fernando, I understand."

"I will call you later when the moment presents."

"Ok, Fernando. I will await your call."

Chapter 13

Fernando walked into Brenda's establishment, *Beautiful Diva's* and he immediately experienced a chill that he had not experienced before. *Something doesn't feel right,* Fernando thought. Fernando knew instantly what to do. "I must begin to pray." That was the only way that Fernando was able to venture forth into the unknown. Fernando knew he must seek wisdom and understanding from the giver of it. Without delay Fernando felt a sense of relief.

"Ok God, I know that there is nothing that will happen today that you and I can't handle together."

"Good morning, ladies," Fernando greeted while entering the salon.

"How are you, Fernando?"

"I am doing well, and how are you all?"

"We are doing well also," stated three of the stylists.

"So what brings you into the salon this morning; did Brenda send you here to check on us?" questioned Delilah, smiling a big radiant smile. Delilah chuckled to herself. Delilah turned to Irene, one of the stylists. "It wouldn't be the first time that Brenda sent someone to check on us. I remember so vividly, it was a warm summer day in July and Brenda had a lady to come in asking questions about a hair weave. It was later determined that Brenda sent her to spy on us, and report back to her what everyone was doing. Imagine that."

"I can see that. Brenda definitely is a piece of work! I come here, do what I have to do, and go home to my old man. Hmmm!" Irene laughed.

"Perhaps Brenda believes that old saying, 'When the cat's away, the mice will play!'"

"Of course not, Delilah; I needed to conduct some business matters, nothing for you to be concerned about. Is Sally available?"

"Sure, let me get her. Sally," called Delilah as she disappeared into the adjoining back room.

Sally surfaced from the back room. "Hello, Fernando, how are you?"

"I am doing well, Sally. How are you doing this fine summer day?"

"I am doing excellent, couldn't be better. God continues reigning in His authority and He is bringing me into my destiny!"

"Amen, Sally that is indeed true. Do you mind if we speak in the office?"

"Not at all; follow me this way," Sally insisted.

"Sally, I have come here this morning to meet with the potential contractors, *Exquisite Renovations Construction Company.*"

"Oh ok; no problem. You can meet with them right in here."

"Sally, I know that would not be a problem; however, I would like you to ensure that we have the privacy to conduct all the discussions."

"Of course, sir," Sally stated willingly.

"When we are ready for them to inspect the project and the commitment they need to make, I would like you to assist me in showing them around. Brenda shared that she has made you aware of all of the renovations beyond what is printed in the blueprint designs."

"Yes, Fernando, you know how we women are, we have that desire to give it a special feminine touch."

"Of course, Sally, I completely understand. That is why I have no reservations of you being able to assist with bringing it into complete fruition! Sally, I wanted to take the opportunity per Brenda, to thank you for the wonderful job you are performing here. If it were not for you being here during Brenda's injury, I don't know how we would have managed."

"Thanks Fernando, you are indeed kind! Certainly, I will take care of your request; once the men arrive from the construction company, I will escort them here to you."

"Before you go, Sally, how have things been here in the salon?"

"Fernando, everything has been pretty good. I took the liberty of ensuring that all the stylists functioned according to the policies and procedures that *Beautiful Diva's* was established on. Since they know my position and allegiance to Brenda they have not fought against my stance!"

"Thanks Sally, I appreciate you being genuine and working in a Spirit of Excellence! I told Brenda she could depend on you! I was able to discern that!"

"Fernando, it means a great deal to me to hear you say this." Sally smiled. "Now, I will be sure to lead the members of the construction company to you once they arrive."

"Thanks again, Sally!" Fernando waited for about 45 minutes, then Sally escorted in the men from *Exquisite Renovations.*

"Greetings, sir, you must be Mr. Storm. How are you?"

"It's Mr. Sexton, and I am doing fine. And you are?"

"Pardon, I'm Mark Townsound, and I apologize for my tardiness, I had a flat tire and had a difficult time and was held up for about 30 minutes. I usually try to be early for assessments, as I want my potential customers to know that I am serious about my work."

"Alright, Mr. Townsound, thanks for the clarification; that would have been my concern if you hadn't mentioned it."

"Mr. Sexton, if you don't mind I would like to take a look at the project at hand."

"Sure, Sally do you mind showing Mr. Townsound and me around to all the potential projects?"

"Not at all, please follow me, gentlemen."

"Here are the blueprints," Fernando stated, extending his right hand.

"Perfect," stated Mr. Townsound.

There was a two-hour meticulous assessment and evaluation completed concerning the project. "Mr. Sexton, at the conclusion of our evaluation the estimate for the completion of this project will be $55,000. This is a reasonable price, considering we will have to clean up the unfinished business of the previous contracting company."

"Mr. Townsound that sounds like an accurate assessment with all the demands of the pending project, I thank you for your time. I will discuss this information with my wife and if your company is chosen for the work, you will receive a call. How soon will you be available to start?"

"Our company is providing the finishing touches on a major project as we speak. The deadline for that is Monday, so we can begin this project on Tuesday or Wednesday at the latest."

"Thanks, again, Mr. Townsound I appreciate your time. Do have a great day."

"Thanks, you too, Mr. Sexton, and it was a pleasure meeting you."

"Likewise, Mr. Townsound."

Fernando was pleased the meeting was productive and ended the way it did. Fernando was

tickled by the price tag that was granted to complete
the project as well. He knew this would be music to
Brenda's ears as she desired to pay little to nothing.
Not to mention, this assessment was $5,000.00 less
than the original quote of $60,000 by Perkins
Construction. Fernando thought... *God has smiled on*
Brenda yet again! I don't understand but it seems
that money is a big motivator for her. Fernando
knew the moment he mentioned he wished her to
make the final decision concerning the renovations of
her salon, Brenda would be well pleased. Brenda
wanted to make all of the money decisions, and she
wanted to be in control of all money matters.
Sometimes Fernando allowed Brenda to make money
decisions to have an element of peace.

Sugar thought... *Time is passing by quickly, and it seems as though Friday got here before I could turn around twice.* Sugar sighed as she prepared to go to the doctor's office that morning. *Today is the day that I will put an end to my wondering whose child I'm carrying. I remember my mom and grandmother saying that while you carry a child you're training them even while they are growing in your womb. I used to wonder how that was possible but this being the fourth child I am carrying I understand it very well. And it is true. Where is my sister? I am happy that I told her to be here 30 minutes earlier than I actually needed to leave. I know Gloria means well, but most times she runs a few minutes behind schedule. Although she's late, she's very dependable and I can count on her being there for me. So as I work through this challenge, I thank God for her.*

269

The doorbell rang. "Good morning, my dear Sugar, how are you doing this wonderful morning? How did you rest during the night?"

"Good morning, Gloria, I am doing well. How are you? I am doing well now that I have finally arrived here."

"I had so much difficulty leaving the house in a timely manner this morning, as there was a business call that required my attention and I couldn't ignore it."

"I understand Gloria."

"Are you ready, Sugar?" Gloria asked.

"Yes I am, Gloria, as ready as I will ever be."

"Sugar, don't worry, this too shall pass!" Gloria stated with much compassion. "At the conclusion of the test, you will soon receive the results. At that moment your heart will be satisfied and what you require to proceed forward will be available to you."

"Yes, Gloria, you are absolutely right. I thank you as you always know exactly what to say as well as the appropriate time to express it. Well let's go."

Gloria and Sugar arrived in the parking lot of Dr. Peters' office and they noticed Fernando waiting in his vehicle in the adjoining parking space.

Sugar thought... *Seeing Fernando waiting here with so much patience and understanding it brings my life joy and happiness all at once. This happiness radiates in both of our attitudes and countenances; it is no secret how much we care for each other.*

"Good morning," Fernando verbalized while opening my car door.

"Good morning Fernando," Sugar responded with a smile. "How are you? I am well, Fernando, although I am a bit anxious to complete this process."

"Yes, Sugar, the feeling is indeed mutual. I must be candid with you; I have been praying that you are carrying my child. I have been longing for the reality of holding my child. It's partly fulfilled holding my nieces and nephews, but they are not my children. Stanley doesn't deserve a woman like you. He has a treasure, yet he doesn't recognize your true value. He has a diamond that he handles like costume jewelry."

"Good morning." The receptionist gave a friendly smile. "How may I be of assistance to you?"

"I have an appointment this morning," Sugar responded.

"Certainly. Will you please sign in, so I can complete the registration process?"

"Sure."

"Ok, Mrs. Spickley, has any of your information changed?"

"No, there have been no changes since my last visit; everything is current."

"Alright, if you will have a seat, the nurse will collect you in a few moments."

"Mrs. Spickley, good morning. I am Nurse Terry; shall we proceed to the back? How are you doing this fine morning?"

"I'm doing well, Nurse Terry and I would like to introduce you to my dear friend Fernando."

"And how are you, Fernando?"

"I'm doing fine and yourself?"

"I'm doing fabulous. I can't complain, thanks for asking. This procedure should not be lengthy. I will be collecting some DNA from the two of you in the form of blood samples. Next, we'll send the blood samples off to the lab, the blood samples will be screened and it will be determined if Fernando is the father. This should not be painful; I am gifted in the area of collecting blood samples, starting IVs, as well as giving injections."

The blood collection was completed in about 10 minutes. *Wow, that was fast,* Sugar thought, as she witnessed Nurse Terry neatly placing the blood specimens in a bag.

"Ok, I have finished and I hope it met with your approval."

"It was fine," Sugar and Fernando stated in unison.

Sugar and Fernando walked into the waiting room and collected Gloria, and they desired to spend some time alone.

"Gloria, thank you so much for waiting for me," Sugar stated. "How was your wait? Were you comfortable?"

"Certainly, Sugar, it was no problem waiting for you as it was a speedy process. I had enough reading material to keep me occupied and I stepped outside to make a couple of business calls. The time has been productive for me as well."

"I am ecstatic to hear that. Gloria, Fernando and I need some time to be alone. If it's alright, I will have him to drop me off at your house later this afternoon.

"Sugar, of course it's alright, you don't have to ask for permission to visit my home."

"Yes, I understand that, Gloria, but I never want to be inconsiderate. I always like to ask instead of bogarting my way in!"

"Sugar, I am excited and overjoyed to have some time to spend with you again. There is not a day that I don't reflect on you and the jewel you are. You are indeed invaluable."

"Fernando, the feeling is truly mutual. Each time I think of you, I am able to endure with Stanley just a little while longer. It makes my heart glad. I almost feel giddy, like a young school girl with her very first crush."

"Thank you, Sugar; you always know how to reach the full essence of my being! It is amazing when I think about the connection that we share it is spiritual."

"Sugar, what are your plans concerning the results of the test?"

"Fernando, there is no easy answer to this question. They will both place me at a pivotal place; I face a life changing decision either way."

"Yes, Sugar I agree. Please know I am here for you."

"Fernando, I appreciate that. Ever since I returned home from the hospital, Stanley has been very distant. We are not communicating much, and when I try to reach out to him to talk, he simply responds by saying he doesn't have time to discuss it. He has to handle some form of church business."

"Sugar, I can truly relate as I have problems with communicating with Brenda also."

"Fernando, when I asked if he was willing to go for counseling, he looked at me in a condescending

277

way, responding, 'Is it likely that someone well will seek hospitalization? Why would I agree to counseling when I counsel? There is no need for counseling!'"

"Sugar, let's enjoy the time we have together without thinking of anything that will take us to another place outside of the moment we are having with each other."

"Done!"

"Are you enjoying your food, Fernando?"

"Yes, Sugar, I am enjoying this food, but not as much as I enjoy being intimate and making love to you!"

"Thank you," Sugar verbalized with a sexy smile. "Don't ignite a fire that you will not be able to quench, Fernando!"

"Sugar, it's difficult to behold your beauty, warmth, compassion, elegance, and figure and not become aroused. I have been trying to contain myself since being with you in the doctor's office!"

"Fernando, I understand as it is happening to me as well. There is a well of water springing up inside of me, and I am able and willing to allow this ocean to flow freely."

"Sugar, we will have time soon to act on these behaviors uninhibited," Fernando verbalized gazing into Sugar's eyes!

Wow, this man truly melts my heart!

Sugar continued in her plight toward reaching her optimal health. She was cognizant of the possibility that things may not work with her husband and she would be responsible for the financial resources of her family. Sugar had been taught the importance of relying on God first, then herself to sustain their needs. Sugar reflected on earlier teachings of her mother, *"Sugar, darling, please don't tell your man everything regarding money, 'cuz he not gon' tell you."*

Sugar felt like that statement solidified what was going on in her marriage; as she had uncovered Stanley had been putting money away for his purposes without consideration of the household. After that discovery she often wondered what else he had hidden from her. Sugar knew within herself that it would be necessary to provide a satisfactory life for her and her family. Following the surgery and as Sugar re-entered the home after a month of rehabilitation, things in the Spickley household had changed a great deal.

Considering the medical condition she faced, Sugar thought Stanley would have been more compassionate and **accommodating.** Sugar affirmed it was a miraculous recovery, and Stanley had no knowledge whether she would return to her optimal health or not. Stanley had continued the status quo or the norm of life as if Sugar continued being absent or displaced from the household.

Stanley had returned full circle to working on the fundraising events at the church in addition to late night meetings and counseling sessions following the **board meeting.** Sugar remarked within, *Go figure, it seems that there are couples within the church or community with an emergency at least four times a month. Well, I will just allow these things to roll off of me like water off a duck's back. I can't wait until I take this much needed vacation/get away.*

It brought so much joy to my heart when I received the call from Gloria earlier, declaring Samuel's reaction to the trip, "He is elated and says we can make the trip, so let's start packing, girl. I want to see you in a bikini before you deliver my niece or nephew!" I am very happy that I still have about three weeks to recuperate before returning to work. I am beginning to place things into perspective and I realize that I have the ability within to change or shift my reality. I can choose to be the victim or to be victorious. I can't wait until we leave for this trip, it's about a week away!

Beep, beep, beep!

Who could that be? Everyone knows that I don't respond to someone blowing the horn outside. Sugar gazed out the window pulling the draperies back. *Oh, it's the mail carrier, Raymond,* she realized, running out the door.

"How are you, Sugar? I am so glad to see you. I saw your car and I took a chance that you may be home. I wanted to hand deliver this mail to you. Looks like you have quite a few pieces of mail," Raymond stated, handing Sugar the mail.

"Yes Raymond, I appreciate your sense of urgency to get me my mail and it's nice to see you as well. How are Heather and the kids?"

"Oh Sugar, thank you for asking; everyone is doing fine. Ashley had a softball tournament last week and her team won. She possesses very good sportsmanship."

"Wow, Raymond. Please congratulate her for me."

"Will do, Sugar. I would love to chat with you more, but you know I have a bunch of deliveries to make before the close of day. It was wonderful seeing you again. You take care and be blessed," Raymond stated warmly.

"Thanks, Raymond, you have a blessed day as well!"

Sugar flipped through the mail and headed back into the house. Sugar, took in a deep breath in an effort to calm her rapidly beating heart and her shaking hands. Sugar discovered a big brown envelope from Dr. Peters' office, and plastered on the front in big red letters was the heading Open Immediately! Concealed inside the brown envelope was another brown envelope with the paternity test results. The correspondence contained in the envelope indicated Fernando Sexton, father tested, Charlotte Spickley, mother tested, and NIPP unborn child. The end of the correspondence read: It has been determined with 99.9% accuracy that Fernando Sexton is the father.

Sugar thought... *It is a major relief to finally have the answer, to discover whose child I am carrying. Now the bigger question is: What now?*

Sugar decided to call Fernando to share the news with him. "Good morning, Fernando. Is this a good time for you?"

"Good morning, Sugar; give me a few minutes and I will dial you back."

Ring, Ring. "Good morning, this is Sugar speaking."

"Good morning, beautiful, I'm returning your call. How are you?"

"I'm doing well."

"How are you?"

"I'm fantastic, especially since I'm hearing your voice," Fernando stated ecstatically.

"I wanted to share with you that I received the results of the paternity test and you are the father. This is our child that I am carrying. Fernando, I want more than anything now to be reunited with my daughter that I was forced to give away for adoption." Sugar burst into tears!

These feelings have begun to surface all at once!

"Hey sweetie, calm down. Take some deep breaths; it will be okay. Everything will work out. I sympathize with you in the loss of a child, and there is grief and bereavement associated with it. There is light at the end of the tunnel. Your daughter remains alive! I promise you that I will do everything in my power to assure that you will find your daughter."

"Thank you, Fernando, I really appreciate your understanding."

"Sugar, let's celebrate the news of you making me a father. I am extremely grateful! I am eternally indebted to you!"

"Fernando, how do you propose we celebrate?"

"Sugar, don't you worry about that. We will be going away in a few weeks, so that will be the beginning."

The beginning of what? I have not made any commitments to Fernando; I remain married to another. Well, I am not going to consume myself with these thoughts. I will choose to enjoy the moment.

"Well, Sugar I have some good news as well."

"Oh?" Sugar was intrigued.

"I received a monetary bonus today from my employer. I was not expecting it!"

"That is great news, Fernando. How much was it?"

"Sugar, I received $2,000.00 tax free, and in time for our travels to Jamaica. I can't wait to behold your beauty in the evening sunset of the Caribbean!"

"Thanks, Fernando. I look forward to that chapter unfolding with you as well!"

Chapter 14

Stanley abruptly entered the house, slamming the door behind him. "What is going on, Stanley?"

"Nothing that our emergency board meeting will not solve!" screamed Stanley. "I don't understand how he had the audacity to question my integrity!"

"Who is questioning your integrity, Stanley? What are you rambling about?" Sugar questioned.

"One of the deacons called a meeting with our governing board, stating there were some questions regarding the account associated with the fundraising campaign. He further stated he has attempted to express his questions with me as the Pastor and founder of the organization, but I haven't made the proper accommodations to entertain him."

"Imagine that?"

"He has been a member of the church well over 20 years. When it rains, it pours! I will get to the bottom of this!" Stanley stated fiercely.

"Stanley, I can understand you feeling frustrated with the information you have shared. I just ask that you calm down, it's difficult to formulate an effective and practical plan when you are upset. It is better when you are able to think to devise a great strategy," Sugar stated warmly.

"I think you are right, sweetie," stated Stanley, giving Sugar a peck on the lips. "I apologize for my entrance. I appreciate you being understanding."

"No problem, Stanley," Sugar stated. "Remember, Gloria and I will be traveling to Jamaica on Wednesday next week. This is coming at the most opportune time for me. I am feeling much better; matter-of-fact, I am on my way back to my optimal health. I was able to complete my 30-minute workout today. I am happy that I've been able to hit that benchmark for a week now. Stanley, you don't have to worry about our young adults. My mother will be staying here, so you may continue your rigorous schedule. I do not want to inconvenience you in any form," Sugar stated sarcastically.

"Thank you, Sugar, I appreciate your effort to ensure the work of the Kingdom of God continues without being disturbed."

Sugar thought, *Stanley has shown me the type of personality he possesses, as well as the type of man he is! The way that Stanley behaves, people would think that I conceived these children independently. All people have to do is take into*

291

consideration the labor Stanley contributes to the lives of our children. During baseball and track season, Akeem would often ask, "Mom, why it is that Dad didn't make it to my game?" I would always give some decent excuse that placed Stanley on a pedestal. I never wanted our children to view him negatively. One thing is for certain, children understand and discern far more than we, as parents, are aware!

Sugar called Gloria and relayed the results of the paternity test. "Hey girl, how are you doing this fine evening?"

"Sugar, I am doing absolutely wonderful! Just finished the final meeting with my last client, so I am ready to relax, unwind and have a glass of wine!"

"Well, I am pleased to hear that. Gloria, I have received the results of the paternity test."

Gloria interrupted the pause, "And?"

"I am carrying Fernando's baby."

"Ok, Sugar you have been able to bring closure to the situation. How are you feeling?"

"Gloria, I have been having mixed emotions. I take full responsibility for my position as I understand the facts of life. There was always the possibility of our lovemaking producing a child. I am relieved to know, now to inform Stanley and allow the chips to fall where they may."

"Sugar, one thing is for certain: you love Fernando and it isn't just a casual affair. Sure everyone will not understand this path of your journey. There is a reason for everything. Right now it may be unclear why you are at this place, as time moves on it will be revealed. Who is to say what happiness and joy this child will bring to edify your life and existence? These are the things we have to leave to God, for he understands and knows the true essence of every situation and circumstance. God reveals mysteries beyond the comprehension of man!"

"Gloria, I appreciate you saying that. Yes, Fernando and I share a very special relationship, one of true love!"

"Sugar, are you ready for our trip to Jamaica?"

"Gloria, I am indeed ready for this trip, and I am feeling that this will be a monumental trip for me. I am expecting something great to unfold during this trip. I have yet to discern what it is, but I am sensing expectation in my spirit."

"Well, Sugar I must say it sounds like a blessing and I receive it in my spirit totally! May God manifest the blessings pertaining to this trip, in Jesus' name!"

Sugar thought... *There is an adage that says, "Time flies when you are having fun." Well, I would challenge this adage today; even when things are difficult, time flies! It seems that it was some weeks ago when we planned to travel on this vacation getaway and today is the day of travel. Not that I am not ready; it is long overdue and I need to get away and relax. I haven't taken the time to discuss with Stanley concerning the paternity of the child. I will face that when I return, I decided to have some element of peace before traveling on this trip. Although the trip is for two weeks, I have packed three bags, which means I will have to pay for an extra bag if Fernando packed more than one bag, but it's ok.*

"Sugar, darling have you finished packing?"

"Yes, Mom. I believe I have everything that I need. I want to make sure that I have all I require for this trip."

"Gloria is downstairs."

"Really, when did she arrive?"

"About ten minutes ago."

"Wow, I didn't even hear the doorbell. I was in my zone, listening to music, and concentrating on packing."

"Sugar, I want to be sure you will not miss your flight."

"Mom, we have more than enough time for the flight; you know how Gloria has a tendency to run behind schedule?"

"Of course, I know that all too well."

"Well, I took her tardiness into account when planning this trip and to sweeten the deal, I received a notification from the airline that our flight would be leaving approximately one hour later. I failed to mention that detail to Gloria."

"Ok Sugar, I understand that! Glad that you took the liberty of ensuring everything was placed in order. I am happy that you asked me to be here in your absence."

"Mom, I am ecstatic and filled with joy that you accepted. I know Akeem and Jessica are thrilled you will be here with them. I am sorry to say this, but there is almost a non-existent relationship with

Stanley. It's almost like he just tolerates them. Mom, I don't know if our marriage will survive. I don't have the same amount of energy and motivation I possessed when we first married. When we married, I always thought our marriage would last forever. I realize more than ever that pregnancy is not a reason to remain in a loveless marriage. At this stage of my life I welcome peace and tranquility. I choose to live an abundant life! I realize and accept that I have a factor in shaping my reality and expanding my world view."

"Sugar, I have always admired your strength to always soar like the eagle. To make lemonade out of lemons. Everyone doesn't possess that ability, as I struggled in that area. I had dreams and goals of becoming a lawyer, but I married your father at a young age, and then I had the responsibility of rearing you all. William was from the old school of thought, stagnation, and he believed that women belonged in the house and not in the workforce. He always stated the Bible instructs that as the breadwinner, he was obligated to provide for his family as the man. 'I am the head of this house and that settles it! That is why I always engrained it in your and Gloria's head that the sky is the limit. Also, that you not allow others to place limits on you."

"Yes, Mom I always remember you telling us. Another famous quote was, 'You cannot expect to soar with the eagles if you eat with the chickens!' Mom, I love you and although we have had our challenges, I am happy that God placed us together. Well, let me get down to Gloria; it is time that we must head to the airport."

"Good morning, Gloria, how are you?"

"Girl, I have been waiting down here for close to an hour now."

"Stop exaggerating, you have been here for no more than 20 minutes!"

Viewing the suitcases Mom and I were carrying, Gloria continued, "Ok, perhaps you have a point. How long are you planning to stay in Jamaica?"

"Haha, funny, Gloria!"

"Sugar, I am not being facetious. Three bags? What did you pack?"

"Gloria, in case you don't remember I am pregnant; I have to make sure that I have everything I could possibly need on this trip!"

"Ok, dear, I packed very light and I was able to get everything into one suitcase."

"Really, Gloria, how did you manage that?"

"Sugar, I packed about six pairs of shorts, 12 tops, and swimwear, I figured I will be able to change it up enough to appear I have 14 days of outfits. I am traveling with Samuel and we are beyond the stage of 'dressing to impress.'"

"Gloria, what about a dress for an elegant evening out?"

"Of course I packed my hot little red number that should suffice for that occasion."

"Sugar, you have always taught me the value in always packing one elegant piece; I have not forgotten."

"Alright, shall we go?"

While Sugar and Gloria headed to the car, Stanley pulled into the driveway.

"Good morning Sugar, I was hoping to catch you before you left the house."

"Good morning, Stanley."

"Sugar, I know that we haven't been able to talk lately."

"Yes, Stanley it appears you have been pulling away from me. I don't wish to discuss this now. I have a flight to catch and wish to leave with an element of peace and tranquility."

"Yes, Sugar, I don't wish to cause you grief. I wanted to give you this." Extending his hand, he gave her a white envelope. "I wanted to provide you with some spending money. Enjoy your vacation. Please return quickly back to me." He pulled Sugar close to him and planted an enormous kiss softly on her lips.

Wow, I never anticipated this. What is happening? He has given me money for the trip? What is he trying to do? Is he trying to cloud my judgment? Why is he now trying to reach out to me? Is this genuine, as I am traveling today?

"Thanks, Stanley, I appreciate that. I am expecting to enjoy my vacation."

Gloria wasted no time addressing Stanley's behavior, "Sugar, what was that all about?"

"Gloria, I have no idea, I am as astonished as you are! I am having trouble conceptualizing his intent, I am unsure if it is genuine."

"I understand completely, Sugar. I'm sure I would have my reservations as well. So how much did he give you?"

"Gloria, it's one thousand dollars in this envelope, ten crisp $100.00 bills!"

"Wow, Sugar!" Gloria stated in amazement.

"Gloria, it's important now that I stay focused. I am going to enjoy this time away and finalize my plans regarding this shift in the present chapter of my journey."

"Fernando, I have been calling you for the past five minutes," Brenda stated abruptly entering the bathroom.

"Brenda, I didn't hear you; you know it's difficult hearing things in the shower."

"What is it?"

"I was just thinking... how will I make it to my final appointment with my orthopedic doctor on

Wednesday, being you are traveling out of town today?"

"Brenda, how have you been getting to your appointments? Do you remember telling me you didn't want me to accompany you to your appointments, as I was ignorant to the medical terminology? Brenda, it was a slap in the face when you verbalized it as I have been working as an EMT/paramedic for the past 20 years."

"Fernando, you know I was playing when I made the statements concerning you not being medically astute. Sally has been taking me to my appointments, but she has a family emergency she is presently attending to. She will not be available to take me."

"Brenda, how was I to know you were not serious? You have shut me out countless times; why would it have been different this time? Brenda, I am sorry, but I will not be available Wednesday. As you are aware, my traveling begins today."

"Ok, fine Fernando, it seems that you continue being selfish; although, I continue going through pain and agony. You have planned a trip to travel during the time when I must embark on returning back to work. Do you realize how much responsibility owning a salon is? Of course you don't, as you have never acquired the skills of operating one. Sure, you may desire to negate this statement, notating the times you have shared in some of the responsibilities and duties of the day-to-day operations of the business."

"Brenda, I can't believe you have the audacity to verbalize I am being selfish when I have always stepped in per your request! I was just there meeting and negotiating with *Exquisite Renovations*," Fernando snapped. "Brenda, I refuse to allow your

306

shenanigans to cause a roadblock and prevent a blissful vacation. I choose to continue making this a great day!" Fernando stated making his exit out of the home.

Brenda concluded there was some soul searching that was needed during this time while Fernando was away. Brenda had begun having some reservations about being married. Brenda began to question if she made the right decision by marrying Fernando. Brenda always suspected she would be successful, and felt she had made it without the help of anyone. Fernando was so accommodating before, but it seemed things shifted when Brenda told him she had aborted their child. Brenda thought... *Don't I have the exclusive right to have control over my body? Of course I do! One thing is for sure, I am not willing to compromise! Life goes on, one step at a time. So if I decide to terminate this marriage, I will be well able to take care of myself.*

Fernando thought... *At last, I am on my way!* "Whew!" Fernando stated as he inhaled a deep breath. Fernando wondered to himself... "*Must we continue engaging in these one-sided dialogues? Is there any hope for us? Today's encounter seems to be the norm in our home these days. Well, I will put that out of my mind right now. Today I choose to have happiness and joy. I truly believe happiness is a state of mind and we can choose to rule our day. Jamaica here I come!*"

Chapter 15

Fernando declared, "Boy, time flies!" Glancing down at the stereo clock in his Cadillac Escalade, he added, "I have about an hour and half before the plane leaves. I am ready for this vacation and I need it like never before. I am so frustrated right now; can't wait to taste the abundance of the fruitful land of Jamaica. Let our journey begin!" Fernando made it to the departing gate in record time. *That was the quickest time spent through airline security; it must have been a record, but I don't have any complaints.*

"My, my, my, ma'am, is anyone sitting here?"

Sugar looked up before responding, "Fernan—" Before she was able to utter his complete name, he scooped her up out of the seat and planted a long, sweet, soft kiss on her lips. Sugar was speechless for a moment. Then uttered, "Wow, Fernando, I really needed that!"

"Have you been waiting here long?"

"No, actually we just completed passing through airline security. It seemed there were many checkpoints along the way that hindered the process. Don't misunderstand me, I want to be safe, but sometimes it can be an inconvenience! But, let's not focus on that; how was your trip over here?"

"It was fine, Sugar, but I had some difficulty leaving the house."

"Oh?"

"Yes, Brenda wanted to discuss her transportation to her orthopedic appointment, desiring to involve me in the process. Imagine that!"

"Well, Fernando, from what I have heard of Brenda, she sounds to be very self-absorbed as well as selfish. I have yet to meet her so it is difficult to form my own opinion concerning her character. I can relate to being caught by surprise with Stanley before leaving the house. I was uncertain of how to define the situation, as I was leaving, he entered the driveway and hurriedly jumped out of the car, handing me an envelope with money for the trip."

"Really, Sugar?"

"Yes."

"If I remember correctly, didn't you tell me he was keeping money separate from the household?"

"That's exactly what I told you."

Their conversation was silenced when the announcer spoke.

"Good afternoon ladies and gentlemen, it is time to begin boarding Flight 77777, service to Ocho Rios, Jamaica. We will begin boarding zone one, our priority members. Please begin forming a line to my right."

Fernando grasped Sugar's hand and they walked hand-in-hand and approached the boarding area of the plane.

Sugar thought… I feel so protected, safe, and secure at this moment. I feel that I could face anything without difficulty and be alright. Fernando has a way about him that is almost regal. He commands attention.

Fernando and Sugar entered the plane and realized Gloria and Samuel were already nestled in the seats adjacent to theirs.

"Hello, y'all ready for a blissful vacation?"

Gloria was the first to answer, "I am expecting a wonderful time. I am looking forward to learning more about the culture and viewing the sites. I envision walking along the sunset and moonlight beaches allowing the clear blue water to ride across my bare feet. I am also looking forward to some romance with my King."

Samuel agreed. "Darling, all those things sound wonderful. Fernando, what are you looking forward to?"

"I am in expectancy of all Jamaica has to offer me and I am open to what lies ahead! I am embracing this journey and I'm happy to have some undisturbed time with my love, Sugar."

Sugar thought... *I love the romance and compassion that Fernando shows. This is an area of starvation with Stanley. Being with Fernando is so refreshing and rejuvenating. He shows his love for me with confidence of not being concerned with the thoughts, expressions, or opinions of others. That was a very delectable meal and drinks we received and from the looks of things, everyone in our seating area appears relaxed. In my observation many people were sleeping. When I'm with Fernando I feel relaxed and uninhibited, and I have the willingness to share my whole being with him. We have such a connection, even when we are separated I can feel his spirit and know when something is wrong. The meal and the ambience of being on the plane has proven to be both enticing and erotic.*

Fernando moved his right hand in between Sugar's thighs, and she opened wider to receive him and was filled with absolute pleasure and delight. Sugar contained herself, and was immobilized from screaming as she normally did.

Sugar thought... Wow, we are off to a great start! After experiencing that dessert, I was ready for a nap, but before drifting off to sleep it is necessary to thank Fernando for the perfect beginning to our vacation. Sugar planted a long passionate kiss on Fernando's lips. Sugar thought... *I was feeling more alive in every part of my physical body. Love is something powerful, and it is a beautiful thing!* Sugar was awakened by an announcement:

"This is Captain Ebony speaking. We will be landing on the island of Jamaica in the next 20 minutes. The weather is 70 degrees Fahrenheit, a beautiful sunny day. Thank you for flying with us and do enjoy your stay in Ocho Rios."

Now, the next item on the agenda is collecting our luggage and then on to the resort, Sugar thought.

Gloria, Samuel, Fernando and Sugar entered the room of the resort and we surveyed our environment to ensure that our room possessed the amenities promised. We were promised two master bedrooms with king sized beds, Jacuzzi tubs, showers, a full kitchen, including stove, refrigerator, and washer/dryer. We ensured the bathrooms were clean and the beds were clean as well. We flipped the covers back and surveyed the sheets.

Sugar thought... *I must admit I am allergic to germs! For that reason, when traveling I always bring cleaning supplies to be sure that the room meets my expectations. I have been known to bring sheets as well and request the beds be stripped before entering the room. I didn't go through those extremes since we were traveling internationally, but I was*

assured by the concierge that the cleanliness of the
rooms was paramount here.

We continued our survey and ended on the screened-in balcony, taking deep breaths of clean, crisp air, inhaling and exhaling. Our balcony overlooked the ocean, it was the most transparent, clear, blue water.

"What a beautiful sight to behold! Ocho Rios, the name in Spanish meaning eight rivers, refers to the eight rivers of this island, which is absolutely wonderful! The ocean has such a calming, tranquil element. I love being around it as it gives such an intense sense or feeling of peace and serenity," Sugar stated.

We enjoyed the balcony so immensely that we accepted our dinner there. We returned inside to retire for the remainder of the evening. Gloria browsed through the activities catalog, highlighting the various activities that were available on the island.

"Hey guys, look at these gorgeous pictures of Dunn's River Falls; I think it would be enjoyable hiking up these falls. What do y'all think?"

Sugar stated, "It sounds good to me."

"Hey, I'm open to anything," Samuel verbalized.

And Fernando stated, "Count me in."

Sugar thought... *One thing I appreciate about Fernando is he doesn't seem hard to please. If Stanley were here he would have a hundred questions concerning this excursion!*

Gloria continued, excited with the positive response. "There is the Blue Hole where we are able to jump into the water; Turtle River Falls and Gardens; there are also tours available that will allow us to delve into the rich culture and history of the island of Ocho Rios. It looks like there will be enough activities for us to enjoy for the fourteen days of our visit here. I am very excited that we decided to come here."

Fernando and Sugar were awakened by a knock on the door. "Who is it?"

"It's me, Sugar," Gloria stated on the other side of the doorway.

"What are you doing here so early, Gloria?" Sugar questioned while opening the door and pulling her robe together simultaneously. "What time is it, Gloria? I am a bit tired after the travels. Gloria, I thought we would be relaxing today," Sugar stated in a low voice, careful not to wake Fernando, as he had drifted off to sleep.

"Sugar, it is about 9:00 a.m., time for you to rise and shine!"

"Girl, do you know that we were pretty busy last night, throughout the night, we had approximately five rounds. It was a juicy marathon of passionate lovemaking! You know what type of effect Fernando has on me. I was thinking that you and Samuel were getting busy as well!"

"Sugar, yeah we had about one round before going to bed, but you know how I am when visiting a new place, I want to explore."

"Yeah, Gloria I know how you are when it comes to new adventures. But let's just take it easy today and we can start with the itinerary you devised on tomorrow. I just want to enjoy some free time with Fernando."

"Ok girl, well I think Samuel and I will just go

out and walk along the beach or something. I will give you the alone time that you need."

"Gloria, I appreciate your understanding as always."

"Sure, Sugar, you know I am always here for you."

Over breakfast Fernando and Sugar exchanged dialogue concerning the plans for their unborn child. "Sugar, as you know I deeply love and care for you."

"Yes, Fernando, as you know the feeling is mutual."

"Sugar, what are your plans concerning us?"

"Fernando, I would like you to be there for the

baby; I would love to be with you exclusively. There are many things that I need to place in order before we can venture out and confess our love to the world. I want both of us to be totally free and uninhibited. First and foremost, I must be careful concerning the decisions as they impact my children. I don't want them to know that their mother has been having an affair. So let's take our time. What are your plans concerning your marriage with Brenda?"

"Sugar, my marriage with Brenda has run its course; it's just a matter of time. She has already proven she doesn't love me, instead she tolerates me. She is not open to counseling concerning our issues. Matter-of-fact, she has stated there isn't anything in our marriage that needs repairing from her lenses. How do you convince an individual an issue needs resolving, when they don't acknowledge the issue? I'm fighting a losing battle, and frankly, I am ready to turn in my boxing gloves. Sugar, you are the one that holds my heart. After all, you are carrying my unborn child. I am thrilled you have chosen to keep our baby, and I don't take it for granted or take it lightly. You have proven both your love and devotion for me. I am ecstatic we have this time and we have the freedom of being together freely without boundaries.

"Yes, Fernando I feel the same way."

"Sugar, it was so amazing all of the things we have learned on this tour of the island of Jamaica, Ocho Rios," Gloria stated while taking a bite of her Curry Shrimp. "It was breathtaking when our tour guide enlightened us that Dunn's River Falls are 183 meters, and we can actually climb the falls," Gloria continued.

Sugar thought... *Gloria loves adventures as well as history, so she is truly in her zone and element. I always enjoy being accompanied by Gloria; she has a special way of interacting with various people, no matter their culture, race, or socioeconomic status.*

Gloria continued, "We further discovered Ocho Rios is located in the parish of St Ann, garden parish, on the north coast of Jamaica. Ocho Rios was originally termed Las Chorreras, meaning, 'Bay of waterfalls.' Our tour guide further confirmed there are actually seven rivers, Cave River, Don River, Great River, Llandovery River, Pedro River, Roaring River, and White River. It was refreshing having this tour scheduled in the absence of cruise ships, as we were delighted by the personalized attention. We were the only couple on the tour and our tour guide accommodated us by taking our pictures for us.

Tomorrow we will begin our itinerary, visiting the Turtle River Falls and gardens and then Dunn's River Falls. Can't wait to see the luminous lagoon at night. I'm sure that will be radiant! The other areas of interest during this trip are Coyaba River Garden and Museum, Eden Falls at Ruins Restaurant, and Fern Gully, which contains over 500 species and foliage only contained in the Rain Forest. This is a wonderful trip, rich in culture and heritage."

"Sugar, thank you for inviting us to join you all on this journey."

"Gloria, you are most welcome, wouldn't like to share this journey with anyone other than my one and only. Gloria, you have always been there for me."

"Sugar, you have always been there for me as well. God smiled on us when he joined us as sisters."

Sugar thought... *What a fascinating and blissful time spent in Jamaica. It was wonderful company with Fernando, Gloria, and Samuel during this stage of my life's journey. I especially enjoyed having the one-on-one time with Fernando. I am more assured than ever that Fernando and I could truly stand the test of time. I believe we have a future together. There is an adage that states, "People come into our lives for a reason, a season, or a lifetime." I believe Fernando is here for a lifetime, for the long haul! As I reflect on my most recent journey to Jamaica, it is as if I could hear my mother speaking, "Sugar, when you have something to talk about, no matter how touchy the subject, always sit down and discuss it; that's what a true lady does." Well, there's no time like the present to deal with the matters at hand.*

"Stanley, Stanley!" Sugar hollered almost in a scream.

"Yes, Sugar, I'm here."

"It is urgent that we speak now; there are some things that need to be addressed."

"Okay, I'm listening." Standing in the middle of the floor, positioning himself to state, "I am in a hurry, there are other things that command my attention right now."

"Stanley please, would you sit down with me on the couch?"

"Sugar, will this be long? I was preparing for a meeting."

"Stanley, I will try to make it as brief as possible! I don't really know how to say this other

327

than to simply express how I feel. It's difficult, but I've run away from confronting this issue far too long. We have been living together under the umbrella of being married to the church and the outside world; however, it has been many years since I have felt like your true partner.

Daily we both go about our occupations separately, this marriage is truly loveless, Stanley. I can't even remember the last time you touched me intimately and affectionately. I have questioned that several times, and appealed to you concerning my need for compassion, touch, and intimacy. I feel my request has fallen on deaf ears and it appears there isn't a desire to fulfill these needs. Stanley, you are always focusing on the tenets of the Bible, but doesn't the Word command the husbands to show their wives benevolence? There have been countless times when I wanted to be held by you, to be frank and candid; I wanted to make love to you, and you denied me. Stanley, I have requested we seek counseling several times, but you have continued to stand against it. I have made the decision that I am not willing to continue living my life this way. I have decided to make a U-turn in my journey. I wish to sever/terminate our marriage!"

"Sugar, that decision seems so final. Is there any room for compromise?"

"No Stanley, I don't wish to entertain that notion. By the way, I will be leaving in the morning traveling to Pennsylvania to find my oldest daughter."

"Sugar, what are you talking about? What older daughter?"

"Stanley, I gave birth to a baby girl 30 years ago that I was forced to give away for adoption."

"Sugar, why have you chosen to keep this secret from me all these years?"

"Stanley, in many cases it has been difficult engaging in conversation with you and this subject has been very challenging for me to deal with. It still hurts that my heart and body have been separated from my daughter. Let's acknowledge the elephant in the room; you have failed to show me compassion, Stanley. I have already seen an attorney and the divorce process has begun, and you will soon receive the information concerning the hearing proceedings."

"Wow, Sugar darling, it seems that you have everything mapped out."

"Yes, Stanley. It was a process but I am clear this is the end of our journey together as Mr. and Mrs."

"So, what about the baby; will you be seeking financial support for our child?"

Sugar contained herself, she took a big swallow, and it felt like her throat was closing and she couldn't speak again. **Sugar thought...** *The moment of truth has surfaced all at once!*

"Sugar, shall I believe due to your silence that you will seek financial assistance from me?"

I must get myself together before speaking; I must be careful and choose my words gingerly as this is a very delicate subject, Sugar thought.

"Stanley, this is difficult to verbalize. I have been seeing someone else, and our relationship began as a friendship and later developed into intimacy. Stanley, this relationship blossomed into something great. Due to our loveless marriage, I was constantly at a loss of intimacy, and I would practically beg you to invest the amount of time into our marriage you were investing in the church and community. Don't you remember the countless times I pleaded with you for us to have counseling, some intervention from a professional removed from our relationship? Each time this subject matter was introduced, you would speak of your professionalism and ability to handle our marriage. Stanley, I realize I have been abused by you emotionally, mentally, and financially."

"Sugar, am I the cause of you engaging in an extramarital affair? Did you not make that choice to do so?"

"Stanley, answer one question for me, before I qualify your questions with an answer. Can you candidly say there has been no infidelity on your part during our marriage?"

"Sugar, we are not discussing me, as I didn't bring a bastard child into our marital home!"

"Really, Stanley? A bastard child? Is that how you truly feel?" Sugar was furious. "Stanley, I am done; there is no further discussion needed! Please sleep in the guest bedroom until we dissolve of our assets."

Sugar thought... *The nerve of Stanley! I have been in this marriage far too long. It is obvious that he feels he is justified in the treatment he continues offering me! Well, I have faced this situation head on!*

Gloria, Doreen, and Sugar met at the checkpoint of the United Airlines station. "Good morning, you two. How are you doing?" Sugar questioned ecstatically.

"We are doing wonderful!" they answered in unison.

"How are you, Sugar?"

"I am doing wonderful, and happy this time is finally here when I begin the search to find my daughter. Fernando wanted to accompany me on this trip, but since Stanley and I have decided to terminate our marriage, I didn't want to cause any speculation until the divorce process ends completely. Speaking of Stanley, Gloria, there is something I would like to share with you later when we have a moment."

"Sure, Sugar. Don't tell me he has been up to those shenanigans again?"

"Gloria, you don't even have to ask." They both excused themselves from their mother. "Gloria, Stanley had the audacity to call my child a bastard child when it was revealed that he was not the father.

When I asked if he could admit that there was no infidelity on his part, he completed disregarded me and turned the tables. I am so tired of going through this! I don't understand how I arrived at this place in my journey, but there is light at the end of the tunnel. There is a brighter day! This too shall pass!"

"Yes, Sugar those are all positive affirmations and necessary when we are passing through difficult times. I remain here for you, Sugar."

"Yes, Gloria that continues being confirmed by your actions."

"Mom, you will be so happy to know that I was able to get in touch with Aunt Nancy and she will be meeting us at the airport. How long has it been since you've seen your sister?"

"It's been about ten years now since I have seen her," Doreen stated solemnly. Doreen thought... *How will I be able to share with Sugar what has driven*

my distance from my sister? I have longed for time

to spend alone with my daughters in search of my

granddaughter. What will this journey truly unfold?

Made in the USA
Middletown, DE
08 April 2022

63702578R00189